RETURN TO FREETOWN

BY DAN ESIEKPE

Order this book online at www.trafford.com/07-1530
or email orders@trafford.com

Most Trafford titles are also available at major online book retailers.

Note for Librarians: A cataloguing record for this book is available from Library
and Archives Canada at www.collectionscanada.ca/amicus/index-e.html

Printed in Victoria, BC, Canada.

ISBN: 978-1-4251-3829-5 (sc)
ISBN: 978-1-4251-3830-1 (e)

*We at Trafford believe that it is the responsibility of us all, as both individuals
and corporations, to make choices that are environmentally and socially sound.
You, in turn, are supporting this responsible conduct each time you purchase a
Trafford book, or make use of our publishing services. To find out how you are
helping, please visit www.trafford.com/responsiblepublishing.html*

*Our mission is to efficiently provide the world's finest, most comprehensive
book publishing service, enabling every author to experience success.
To find out how to publish your book, your way, and have it available
worldwide, visit us online at www.trafford.com/10510*

Trafford rev. 6/26/2009

 www.trafford.com

North America & international
toll-free: 1 888 232 4444 (USA & Canada)
phone: 250 383 6864 ♦ fax: 250 383 6804 ♦ email: info@trafford.com

The United Kingdom & Europe
phone: +44 (0)1865 487 395 ♦ local rate: 0845 230 9601
facsimile: +44 (0)1865 481 507 ♦ email: info.uk@trafford.com

10 9 8 7 6 5 4 3

*To Brother John... for rising up to the challenge...
to "father" us all... when the old man's head rested
on the bosom of earth – so prematurely!*

*..And to Bridget....for providing the "pillow" and the
"ripening breast" whose "every rise and fall"
made the difference.*

Cover Design by Ovie Esiekpe

Chapter 1

SQUADRON LEADER IKEKE

I T WAS PITCH-DARK when the three Alpha jets took off from the only runway that served both civil and military traffic at the Lungi International Airport that morning. As they broke through the early morning harmattan haze into the clear serenity of high altitude, Wing Commander Akassa, came through on the squadron's attack frequency.

"Eagle One... reporting forty thousand feet..." "Roger. Confirmed. Eagle Two ditto forty thousand feet"

"Eagle Three here... Confirming forty thousand feet...." as the clear voice of Squadron Leader Martin Ikeke came through the ether.

Altitude had been a major issue at the briefing that morning. Located at an isolated foliage towards the Lunsar end of runway 001 of the air-port, the briefing tent was on high operational security alert that morning. The Lungi - airport based ECOMOG Air Task Force had been in isolation and on very high alert since the "Operation Buffalo" push by Area Fada's National Patriotic Front of Liberia(NPFL) army towards Monrovia.

As elements of the 201 squadron filed into the briefing tent that morning, an oppressive hush descended on the squadron. Unlike the small talk and chatter in the mess the previous night, everything about the tent had become deliberate, serious and clinical; with the humming of the overhead projector that provided the source of light in the tenth amplifying the feeling of foreboding. Presently, the Task Force Intelligence Officer, a young Wing Commander, with a cute moustache and a surgeon - type spectacles walked in and put on the shaded lights. The lights illuminated large maps of Liberia. The pilots all drifted towards the maps, taking in huge relief maps of Monrovia, Painesville, Harpel, Buchanan port, Gbarnga, Kakata, Tubmanburg, the Po River.

"Ten... shun!" Everyone froze as Group Captain Peter Shugaba stepped in.

"Morning... Gentlemen... Lanre... Lets go" beckoning to the Task Force Intelligence Officer.

"Gentlemen, two weeks ago... our man Area Fada launched an all – out offensive against our forces on the ground in Liberia. This time, they are supported by newly acquired Armored Personnel Carriers..APCs for short, batteries of SAM – 7 missiles, some refurbished Tiger tanks and long range artillery... For the first time, Monrovia, the capital city has come within range of Area Fada's forward locations... infact, a major street market in Monrovia suffered a direct hit yesterday. Civilians have been fleeing Monrovia and environs... and the sense of panic has been bad for morale... including morale of our own troops."

There was dead silence as he continued. "Unfortunately, the extent of damage and the severity of the challenge from Area Fada has been exaggerated a thousand – fold by a private mobile radio station. The radio station... gentlemen operates on 17.6mhz on the amplitude modulated band. We have very reliable intelligence reports to the effect that the station has also been serving as a command and control centre of sorts by relaying tactical communications to ground forces from Area Fada's headquarters in coded Liberian slangs...."

The Intelligence Officer paused for effect; and turning to the illuminated mock-up of the map of Liberia, he continued.

"I will now take you through the maps... (stabbing on the map) here locations of our forces... Here in Gbanga... the last known location of the private radio. There are some friendly forces, elements of the United Liberation Movement of Liberia (ULIMO) in forward positions located to the South-East of the Po River here...",stabbing a presentation pointer at the green markings of the Po River on the mock-up. He looked up at the now very quiet Briefing Room briefly and continued.....

"The rest of the terrain all the way to the border with Sierra-Leone... into Daru, Zimmi... Mayanga and the Manu River bridge are all enemy territory... heavy movements of Revolutionary United Front of Sierra Leone (RUF) reinforcements into Liberia have been reported... Any questions so far?"

"Not yet!" Squadron Leader Martin Ikeke blurted out... more to relieve the tension... as chuckles went round the Briefing Room. At that point, Group Captain Shugaba, ECOMOG Air Task Force Commander took over.

"Gentlemen... your task this morning is two – fold... One... you will tune into that his bloody "Radio Liberia" frequency... 17.6mhz A.M. and home in on the radio station and take it out. I mean destroy it and shut him up... permanently!

Two... , Destroy the supply column of APCs, ferrets, tanks and long-range artillery... their last known positions are in your file... right there in front of you... Gentlemen I repeat... destroy the radio station and destroy the supply column headed towards Monrovia. It is important that you intercept and destroy that convoy..it is part of a heavy reinforce-ment for their Operation Bufallo designed to seize Monrovia.You have to achieve this major tactical objective to save our men in Monrovia from annihilation. As you know, ECOMOG reinforcements to support our men on ground in Monrovia will not be in position until another one week....your role is therefore crucial to relieving the current pressure... so go ahead and give it your best shot. Your total flight time will be just under three hours and....I expect you back early enough for breakfast! Questions?!"

"G.R. Sir!" It was the baritone voice of Squadron Leader Ogaga at the rear of the Briefing Room. He had raised the very question bordering every mind in the room. It was unlike Group Captain Shugaba to end a briefing without detailed description of the target's Grid Reference (GR).

"Correct!" The Task Force commander barked back. "As indicated in your maps and flight plans…" and Group Captain Shugaba proceeded to talk about the mobile nature of the radio station; but gave the last sighted location of the station as Gbarnga; but moving in the direction of Nimba County. He provided the last known co-ordinates and the relevant land marks and paused for questions. The Briefing Room was now extremely tense. Total silence, then, a deep guttural voice coughed for attention.

"Sir! Anywhere beyond Gbarnga will be out of range of the Alphas and therefore suicidal!… We can make it there quite alright… but we will have just barely enough fuel to make it back… That is if we don't run into foul weather and enemy fire!"

The briefing shifted to tactics. The need to fly high altitude to conserve as much fuel as possible and drop down to attack at the last minute. Avoid diversionary targets and curtail evasive manouvres…

That was one hour earlier. Now, at forty thousand feet, the two Snecma engines roared, delivering full thrust of about six thousand pounds. But Squadron Leader Martin Ikeke, flying wingman to the Mission Commander was worried. Two weeks earlier, he had aborted a mission at the last minute due to a faulty ejector seat and he had hardly recovered from the resultant nightmares and premonitions.

Martin Ikeke had trained in Fighter School in Düsseldorf, Germany with the more advanced Alpha A series, the German version of the sub-sonic fighter/bomber deployed exclusively as a light ground attack and battlefield reconnaissance aircraft. The Alpha Jet "A," the 'A' representing "Appur Tactique" for its tactical strike role had an extended range with its drop tank and superior avionics and armaments.

But the ECOMOG Air Task Force's 201 Squadron Alpha version "E" was the French variant, designed as a twin – seater training and light ground support aircraft, hence the "E" for "Ecole" or School. Whilst the Alpha E's maximum altitude of 50,000 feet was just adequate for light regional conflicts, its limited range of just less than Six hundred kilometers at cruising speed and maximum altitude was a major disadvantage.

The Mission Commander's signal brought Ikeke back from his wandering thoughts as he looked up into the very convenient Head Up Displays to read his course bearing and other data. He checked his laser range finder and the inertial navigational unit and locked his radio on the "Radio Liberia, Gbarnga" frequency. The Station had just played the National Anthem and was then playing the first musical notes of the Station Identity. Even as the bleep from "Radio Liberia Gbarnga" became louder, Squadron Leader Ikeke's thoughts wandered back to the challenges of the mission - distance. But for the "Operation Buffalo" push by Charles Taylor's rag-tag army reportedly supported by some foreign regulars and mercenaries, the natural jump-off airports for this mission would have been the Robertsfield International Airport in Monrovia or Spriggs Payne Airfield. But both airports had been hurriedly evacuated the previous week under intense artillery fire from Area Fada's advancing forward recce units. But since dawn air strikes had been very rare during the campaign, Martin Ikeke was banking on the element of surprise to help the accomplishment of the difficult mission.

As the wing aircraft followed the Mission Commander's signal to commence attack descent, Ikeke brought the aircraft down at close to seven hundred kilometers an hour;;and at a 70° dwell angle. With this move, he broke through the clouds into the early morning sunrise and the thick green mangrove foliage underneath.

Squadron Leader Ikeke felt the strong bleep from the radio station as he peered through the windshield to keep the target area in view. Then he saw the antenna. On closer scrutiny he saw the heavily camouflaged Land Rover. He called a clock code direction to his lead aircraft who apparently had not noticed the target and had over-flown it. The Mission Commander noted the target location and ordered a fly-past and a two-pronged return approach. The re-positioning manouvre completed, Ikeke brought the aircraft to tree top level for better visual appreciation, radar avoidance and reduction of the Alpha jet's target profile. He released bursts of cannons to suppress enemy fire, whilst homing in on the cross-hairs of the radio transmitter as he released the Belouga cluster bombs. Suddenly, the station seized transmission as the Alpha fired even more high explosive rocket rounds.

By this time, the heavily camouflaged defensive military deployment around the Land Rover had overcome their initial shock. They opened a barrage of high velocity Oerlikon anti – aircraft fire and some Bofor tracer bullets. Suddenly, he picked a tracking of a SAM – 7 missile fire on his tail... and banged sharply, climbing at the same time to fifty - thousand feet for evasive tactics. He called in his position to the lead aircraft as he saw from his vantage height, the Mission Commander let loose Belouga bombs and rockets, with all his gun pods firing 30mm cannons simultaneously. The whole folliage erupted in smoke, thunder and rubbles. Ikeke swooped down, mopped up and pulled away imme-diately to avoid ricochets from exploding ordnance. As he climbed back to forty thousand feet for the return journey, the frenzy of his evasive tactics had made him oblivious of the low fuel situation in the aircraft. Combined with a noticeable compressor stall which was logged on a previous sortie and very strong head winds, the Alpha jet was burning more fuel than usual. Mid-way on the return leg, the aircraft's low fuel alarm system went off. He rocked his wings to visually communicate his crisis situation whilst breaking operational silence to call in his emer-gency. "Eagle Three... to Base Control... May Day... May Day... May Day... Eagle Three running out of fuel... Sierra... Oscar... Sierra..."he screamed into the headphone.

"Eagle Three... Eagle Three" cracked through the ether as Mission Control acknowledged the distress...

"This is Base control... confirm position..."

He gave his position as he saw the two other mutually supporting fighters fly close to his wing for support. It was similarly dangerous for the support fighters, since their fuel was also low; so they noted his position and pressed on. There was only one option for Ikeke - land the aircraft at the nearest possible airfield. He was already back into Sierra Leonian airspace, over – flying Kailahun, with Tongo Field and Pujehun in view. The nearest airport was an old civilian airstrip that used to serve the bauxite miners at Sieromco, located just after Gbangbantoke and before Mokanj. It was a grass airfield, with a very short runway...

definitely too short a runway for the required landing distance of six hundred meters for the Alpha.

The Alpha was losing altitude very fast now... and was nose – diving. Ikeke deftly, even with the aircraft's free – fall still managed to manoeuvre it over the Kamuni hills, plunged over Kenema towards Karibundu and Pujehun. At the last minute, it dawned on him that making it to the old airfield at Gbangbantoke was out of the question. He recalled that the last ECOMOG Intelligence briefing had reported fierce fighting in Pujehun, so he banked right sharply to put as much distance as possible between the aircraft and Pujehun. With one deep – throated roar and a spluttering cough, the aircraft took its last breath and went into free fall. At that same instance, Ikeke reached for the ejector harness and pulled...

With the loss of radio contact, a hush fell over the whole of Mission Control at the Lungi International Airport. Air Traffic Controllers and other civilian employees at the adjoining airport felt a premonition with the frenzied activities at the Air Task Force base. The Task Force Commander, Group Captain Shugaba immediately sent a coded message to the Commanding Officer of the 115 Composite Battalion of the Nigerian Army at Jui, near Hastings in Freetown. There, the Operations Officer put together a Quick Response, Search and Rescue unit. A Headquarters team of paratroopers on rotation and always on stand-by was quickly mobilized. A section commanded by Lieutenant Timothy Kalu, alias "Agile" boarded a Super Puma attack helicopter for the last known location of the missing aircraft that morning, precisely one hour after the Alpha jet went down.

A squadron of six Super Puma HC1 helicopters had been an essential part of the ECOMOG Air Task Force from inception. The Squadron even arrived the Lungi airport ahead of the main detachment, ferrying essential supplies, moving personnel, deploying and dropping tactical combat units in far and inaccessible forward locations around the

Freetown Peninsula; and daily mail shuttles with Mission Headquarters in Monrovia.It was from this helicopter squadron that the rescue team drew a Super Puma for the urgent mission. The Search and Rescue team, led by lieutenant Timothy Kalu made the last reported co-ordinates of the Alpha jet in forty minutes. Squadron Leader Chris Balli, the pilot of the helicopter, an experienced veteran saw the tell-tale signs of smoking wreckage first. He banked away to give the right wing mounted UPMG gunner a clearer view of the location. The gunner straffed the wreckage perimeter with high explosive, 7.62 rounds ferociously. Squadron Leader Chris Balli repeated the manouvre with the left-wing gunner, bringing the aircraft to a lower altitude.

With no sign of enemy movement or returning fire, the Super Puma settled for a small clearing about two hundred metres away from the crash site and dropped to six feet for the Search and Rescue team to disembark. Squadron Leader Chris Balli, as standard procedure immediately brought the helicopter up again to forty feet, for better all-round target area observation whilst reducing his own target profile and vulnerability. At a signal from Lieutenant Kalu, the Puma rose into the sky and returned back to base. The Search and Rescue team searched through the debris of the Alpha, recovering essential maps and the code book unaffected by the fire; then commenced a systematic combing of the surrounding under-brush. They worked in concentric rings, expanding the diameter of the ring every time. They searched all through the night; and by dawn when they rendezvoused with the Puma for extraction, they had to return to base with the sad news: Squadron leader Ikeke still confirmed Missing In Action, presumed dead.

The platoon of the Revolutionary United Front was on a steady tab-bing towards Pujehun when they sighted the Alpha Jet. The unit was part of the 44 Battalion that had been in battle with Sierra Leonian forces for over two weeks; and their march to Pujehun was a last throw of the dice by the Papay himself to throw the Headquarters Strategic Reserve into the fray. When the Recce Squad saw the fast diving air-craft, they had assumed it was in an attack profile and dove for cover. But as they watched, the aircraft canopy was flung open and the pilot thrown out like a projectile. As the parachute opened, the wind drifted it and the airman towards the foliage where the RUF platoon was in deep cover. The parachute was stuck on a branch of the very acacia tree under which the platoon was hiding, knocking the pilot violently against the tree trunk repeatedly before leaving him hanging with his head upside down.

The Alpha jet meanwhile continued to nose-dive noiselessly for another twenty miles before coming down heavily with a loud explosion.

The RUF platoon commander, captain Mansarray, an experienced veteran and a beneficiary of formal military training and head of his graduating class at the Benguema Military Academy immediately swung into action. The platoon cut loose the parachute and brought down the unconscious pilot; who was bleeding from the nose; and with an appar-ent fractured shoulder and leg. Quickly, he deployed his men in a three layered perimeter defence and administered field medical resuscitation. As soon as he established a pulse and heart beat; and that the pilot was alive, he tried to radio the Papey at Camp Eleven. But the traffic from Puyehun was heavy and he was in a low-lying terrain that obstructed his line of sight. Thirty long minutes of struggling later, he finally man-aged to raise an elated Papay. Papay, immediately saw the invaluable propaganda value of the capture and ordered the platoon back to Camp Eleven. The platoon had marched for only ten minutes when they heard, before sighting the Search and Rescue helicopter. The platoon quickly went into the thick mangrove foliage. With a makeshift harness, they moved the unconscious pilot up and very deep into a tree trunk, had his mouth and legs taped, camouflaged his position… and waited. Twice, the Search and Rescue squad came close; even had an 'O' group meeting under the leafy tree. But the stillness and camouflage of the platoon was so effective,the all-dusk and all night search produced nothing. The platoon resumed its march to Camp Eleven immediately after the dawn return of the Super Puma and the extraction of the Search and Rescue team.

The platoon commander Captain Mansarray quickly set about the task of moving the airman as soon as the ECOMOG chopper departed. The platoon prepared a makeshift stretcher made of bamboo stock and palm fronds and put the now conscious and moaning pilot on it. From his scarce supply of field medicaments, the arm, shoulder,leg and neck were securely bandaged. Finally, Mansarray gave the pilot a shot of morphine which made him light-headed as he floated away into deep slumber. The platoon took turns carrying the make shift stretcher for the long march to Camp Eleven. Ten hours of non-stop march later, the platoon hit the first perimeter defences and Observation Post of Camp Eleven: a series of evacuated and disinfected ant-hills with look-out holes and a network of underground tunnels at the foot of the densely forested Nimini Hills. The password for the day was "Crow". To the initiated, a call and response mimicking of the sound of the crow, finally led to the order to Advance for Recognition… and the platoon commander advanced with a branch of paw-paw leaves to complete the coded recognition ritual… There was a spontaneous air of excitement as the platoon moved deep into the network of tunnels of Camp Eleven to the warm welcome of 'The Papay' himself.

Chapter 2

BRETT DENNING

As the land Rover trundled down the rocky slope towards Tombo, the ever-busy fishing village, Captain Brett Denning looked forward to his weekend rendezvous at the peninsular resort at Tokey. A veteran of the 5th Battalion of the British Parachute Regiment, he was nostalgic that evening about his recall from Kosovo and subsequent briefing at the Ministry of Defence for his training job in Sierra Leone. The Sierra Leone Army's Chief of Operations and members of the British High Commission were there at the Lungi International Airport to receive his six-man training team. The journey across the sea on the ferry boat – The Pompoli – was refreshing, even in the midst of the noise and frenzy of itinerant traders and returning military units.

He had settled down quickly to pursue his mandate: To train the army of the elected and internationally – recognized government of Sierra Leone and build a professional army that could combat the atrocities of and halt the menace and advance of the RUF rebels into the Government – held territories in the country. His second, not often documented objective was the provision of on-ground military intelligence reports for the Ministry of Defence back in London and provision of periodic jungle training opportunities for elements of the British Army. Such jungle training opportunities had been accorded various units of the Parachute Regiment since the commencement of his mission six months earlier. Captain Denning had quickly settled into the Benguema Military Academy, located to the south-east of the capital Freetown. On this friday, he had opted for the lonely, narrow and rocky peninsular road to avoid the traffic and the long drive through the city centre to Tokey. Like many other foreign combatants in Freetown, he had been surprised at the excitement and frenzy of social life in a city gripped in the throes of war.

The ever – present African rhythms blaring from corner shops on the streets, the ECOMOG Soldiers in their Steyr trucks seemingly always on the move, the endless parties in the highbrow Hill Station diplomatic quarters. Yes, The Freetown Golf Club, with its fairways and greens lapping the atlantic ocean... Lumley Beach and Aberdeen - all the night clubs, the alcohol and drugs... and finally the more exclusive peninsular resorts - Lacca Cotton Club, the resorts at Tokey and Number Two River, Mama Beach, York, Sussex. At night, with a dusk-to-dawn war curfew in place, only the military had the rare privilege of movement. That was when the ECOMOG and Sierra Leonian army officers went for their endless dinners and parties; with their mean-looking body guards providing eagle-eyed security coverage.

And then the girls. Gaily dressed in bright African prints and the ever present tight-fitting jeans and t-shirts. Mostly in their teens and early twenties from the hill-top Fourah-Bay College and the Connaught Hospital's School of Nursing. Hardly a picture of a country at war, with easy money to be made from sexually-starved soldiers by young, sexy girls of easy virtue. Not to mention the brisk black market trade in diamonds by returning combatants from the war fronts.

Bored to death by the stiff manners and the gossips of abandoned and desperate High Commission housewives, Captain Denning had become less and less frequent at the numerous Hill Station diplomatic events and High Commission parties. He mingled more and made friends with his gregarious military type – Sierra Leonian and ECOMOG military officers and the white mercenaries. The two legendary mercenaries; Jack, the white South African combat pilot and Ted, the former SAS

Squadron Commander,who served as Jack's wing gunner became his very good friends. Intelligence from them on the battle situation and behind enemy lines was good. Jack flew the Sierra Leone Army's sole Huey attack helicopter with Ted as his wingman and door gunner. With countless sorties into the rebel strongholds, the graphics of the deaths and atrocities of the war were painfully etched on their memories. So were the beautiful girls, the drinks and the unspoiled coastal beaches.

At Tombo, the fishing village, with numerous coloured dug-out canoes, Captain Denning turned right and headed towards Kent village. He looked across Cape Shilling into the horizon, towards Banana Islands, where he had previously spent a fun-filled saturday with Jack and Ted.

The rocky road had reduced the Land Rover's movement to walking pace, when he had the flat tyre. For two hours, he laboured to have the spare tyre fixed. He had successfully taken out the flat tyre with the Land Rover well jacked up. But the struggle to overcome a worn nut tasked all his energies. Even when he padded the wheel spanner, the nut just simply refused to budge. That was when the three men came alongside the Land Rover. They looked like harmless civilians until they revealed the concealed weapons. At gun-point, they shoved Captain Denning aside and searched the vehicle thoroughly, taking maps, binoculars, hand-held radio and service pistol. Then, they led him off the main road, down-hill towards a point by Yauri Bay. There, by the waterfront were three dug-out canoes and more members of the RUF unit. At this point, Captain Denning was more confused than shocked. He could not imagine a rebel unit operating so far away from the war front and so close to Freetown, the capital.

"I am a British citizen... I work for the Sierra Leone Government... I am a Teacher..."

"Shut-up!! We know who you are!", a voice rang out from the mangrove foliage.

He turned to look at the man who came out of the foliage and obviously the leader of the unit; and was truly shocked and afraid for the first time. Officer Cadet Caulker! How? When? Why? Graduate of the

Sierra Leone Military Academy, Benguema. Best graduating cadet at a colourful ceremony only a fortnight ago. Distinguished recipient of the Milton Magai Merit Award. Caulker saluted smartly.

"Sir,Lieutenant Moby Caulker in command Sir.. 7th Marine Commando, RUF. You have to come with us..Sir!" "

"But you… !!"

"Yes! Your former officer cadet. I am a Sierra Leonian… I am entitled to your military education… for your information, over 20% of your cadet officers were RUF members… Anyway, let's go…"

They had Captain Denning's hands and feet tied, and led him into one of the dug-out canoes. The Commandoes paddled all night in silence, a dark silhouette against the dark stillness of the African night. They passed the occasional fishermen with their tell-tale lanterns. Just before dawn, they abandoned the dug-out canoes and marched inland into the Mokanji hills, where they camped for the day. They continued their march in a south-easterly direction the next night, cutting through the Bo-Kenema highway at a lonely spot. That day, they camped at Boajibu; and marched all the way the next night to Camp Eleven.

Chapter 3

MARK BURDEN

CAPTAIN BRETT DENNING'S abduction jolted the entire Sierra Leonian leadership, the British and European communities in Freetown, the British Army Command; and occasioned a frenzy of activities at the Ministry of Defence in London. At the Peninsular Resort in Tokey near Freetown, a long anxious wait by Jack and Ted and their ever present horde of young Fourah Bay College girls soon grew into a panic. They had agreed to meet at 4 p.m. and Aishatu, Brett's tall,slim, silky catch of the previous weekend was ready and waiting when their worst fear was confirmed by an ECOMOG officer who sauntered by. The major, the O.C. Charlie Company, 115 battalion of the Nigerian Army, responsible for security around the peninsular area said he had picked frantic radio traffic to confirm the disappearance of Captain Denning.

Radio intercepts in the two weeks following the abduction of Brett showed significant RUF concentration around Kasare Hills. Subsequent reconnaissance flights confirmed a heavy build up of RUF combatants around the hill. At the Southern end of the hill towards Lake Taiama and the northern end towards Yoribana, heavily fortified encampments were established by aerial surveillance. Following two weeks of intelligence gathering,which established the presence of a Caucasian prisoner in the Kasare Hills camp of the RUF; and very intense parallel planning, the Ministry of Defence received approval to upgrade the status of preparations for a rescue mission to "Amber". This necessitated the movement of men and material to the jump-off positions on the HMS Storm-Conquest anchored on the atlantic ocean, which served as the Forward Operating Base for the mission.

"Here... we go boys... "A" squadron will go in with five Super Pumas to a Drop-off-Point thirty miles North of our target area... here." Captain Sutton paused and looked into the determined faces of the fifty men of the Parachute Regiment selected for the mission. He continued.

"B Squadron... you will fly into the Drop-off Point here at the South also thirty kilometers from the target area... then march all night into your new jump-off-positions... here and here... and here!" stabbing at the map again.

"... "A" Squadron... you will carry on recce patrol and take up positions on this hill here for tactical advantage and with clear lines of fire... just before dawn... Captain Denning is reportedly held in a hut here... He reportedly has a regular routine and uses the nearby stream here for his bath every morning at about 6 o'clock. The attack will commence as soon as you have him covered... Your Task is simple. You will locate, free Captain Denning and inflict maximum damage on the RUF Camp. He repeated the Tasking Statement and re-stated the duration: "Your mission commanders will determine the mission duration. Once Captain Denning is secured, you will call in the Pumas on radio... Call sign again will be a phonetic code - "Kamara".

Gentlemen... you have everything... Rendezvous... your grid references, synchronized timings, extraction procedures... Any questions?"

The helicopter drop was uneventful. So was what proved to be over one hour of steady tabbing. The two squadrons were in position and properly concealed by first light. Dawn revealed a sprawling garrison in physical exercises and drills, all under the cover of the hills and the rain forest. The initial Intelligence estimate of about two hundred RUF soldiers at the camp was obviously wrong. The Mission Commander analyzed the relative strength of the enemy position and called into the

Forward Operating Base for additional air support to be dispatched and vectored on stand-by. Promptly, four Lynx Attack helicopters were dispatched. As the fog of dawn began to thaw, five soldiers came marching downhill towards the stream with a hand-cuffed captive… a white man! The bearded, dishevelled white man looked strange in the African loin cloth "wrapper" that he tied around his waist and chest. There was an instant quiet hush amongst the concealed paratroopers. There was no time to waste. And they might not get a second chance. At a sign from the Mission Commander, three paratroopers lifted 203 rifles and fitted silencers.

In one swift action, they fired and took out the five RUF escorts and charged forward to secure "Captain Denning"; simultaneously calling in the waiting Lynx helicopters. That was when all hell broke loose. The attack caught the camp by surprise as all the RUF perimeter defences and Observation Posts were attacked simultaneously. With the Lynx helicopters flying at tree level and heavily concealed, death came to the camp unexpectedly from all quarters. Within thirty minutes the garrison had been effectively pinned down; and with the Lynx providing covering fire, the paratroopers began an orderly pull back to rendezvous with the Pumas. But the RUF garrison had overcome the initial surprise and its sheer numerical strength began to tell in the ferocity of the returning small arm fire. There was an old Swedish Bofors anti-aircraft battery at the western perimeter of the camp which started providing a very deafening response. In a disorderly roar, the remnant of the garrison charged towards the retreating paratroopers. The RUF soldiers forged through the muddy swamp and stream in hot pursuit all the way to the Extraction Rendezvous with the Pumas. "A" Squadron extracted successfully with a few minor injuries. But as the last of the "B" Squadron made to take-off, Sergeant Mark Burden, Leader of the Section that provided perimeter cover for the extraction RV, jumped in briskly to mount and harness his UPMG to serve as a side gunner during the extraction. It was a standard drill that he had performed so many times in the past in many combat situations. But this morning, just as he had secured the UPMG, the Puma suddenly made a violent left bank as the pilot lifted the chopper to take off and at the same time executing an evasive action... and Sergeant Burden was thrown off-balance and flung out of the Puma. Unhurt, he got up promptly and dashed for the now climbing helicopter. The helicopter swivelled round to direct its front mounted machine guns and canons at the advancing RUF hordes. By that swiveling action', Sergeant Burden again lost his fledgling hold and fell down with a clumsy thud that fractured his left femur. An excruciating pain ran through him as he attempted to get up... and collapsed in agony. The RUF garrison was now fully mobilized as they descended on the Puma with all manner of small arm fire. Suddenly the Bofor anti-aircraft gun pulled out of the thick undergrowth and found the range of the Puma and the supporting Lynx which had run out of ammo at this point. The Bofor was noisier than effective and continued to fire aimlessly, but the noise was scary. At that instant, a rocket propelled Grenade landed in the fuselage of the Puma, with a blinding explosion, spewing blood, mangled flesh and bones. A sharpnel from the grenade struck a hydraulic duct underneath the pilots pedal with a resultant loss of hydraulic pressure. With hydraulic pressure failing, the pilot beat a hasty retreat from the extraction RV; with the rampaging RUF in pursuit

With the dust and smoke of battle now clear, an injured and abandoned Sergeant Burden was captured by the RUF; and ferried in a makeshift stretcher in an all-night tabbing to Camp Eleven. It was a gloomy atmosphere that enveloped HMS Storm Conquest that night. Six dead, nine wounded and one missing!! That was the gloomy terse report that filtered into the Operations Room at the Ministry of Defence in London that night. And Captain Denning? The sad realization that Captain Denning was not at the two Camps the Intelligence people had code-named Camps Alpha and Bravo and the grossly under-estimated strength of the garrison shocked the entire Forward Operating Base. True, there was anticipation of some resistance. It was known that the RUF had packed some significant fire-power on two recent encounters, but a fully-armed and mobilized battalion strength with anti-aircraft perimeter defences! As the Intelligence people grilled the freed "Captain Denning", they were told of a network of trenches running under the hills, the arrival in the last twenty-four hours of massive reinforcement in preparation for a major offensive. "Captain Denning" who turned out to be Christensen Smicer, a Danish aid worker who was abducted on the Bo-Kenema Road the previous week along with his local Sierra Leonian assistants confirmed that he was the only white man in the camp.

Christensen was full of praise for the British Army for his rescue that evening on the BBC's Focus on Africa programme.

Chapter 4

ABENNA DONKOR

THE SLEEPY VILLAGE of Nsesereso, near Fetenta in the Ashanti heartland of Ghana was recognized for one thing. True, they were also noted for cash crop farming with their rich cocoa harvest being sought after year after year in the produce markets of Sunyani and Kumasi. But the village was famous for being home to the one man who brought so much fame and respect to Ashanti culture ; the one with the minstrel's voice, the Court orator extra-ordinaire and the deeply spiritual traditional medical practitioner Nana Kwabena Donkor. Nana Kwabana Donkor, once described by a visiting team of British Royalty as a living human encyclopaedia of Ashanti history, culture and tradition reflected his greatness even in his physical stature. A man with a dark-glowing skin, of commanding built,standing at over six feet, he filled every social gathering with his wisdom, charisma and talent. He was an extremely colourful personality who made his mark in his native Nsesereso before his fame and knowledge spread afar and recommended himself to the ancient Ashanti royal court. He had no western education of any kind; and busied himself tilling the land and the provision of traditional health care which was passed on to him by his father, and his grand – father, before him. Such was his fame, that the documentary on the Asantehene's hosting of the Royal Court of Great Britain gave him more footage than the Otumfuo,the Ashantehene himself. The turning point for Nana Kwabena Donkor came when he was included in the official delegation from Sunyani at the coronation of the Asantehene Otumfuo, The First. In the frenzy of the preparations for the coronation, the official Linguist and Orator had suddenly developed a high fever and sore-throat. With the resultant loss of his voice, the need to get a reliable linguist at that eleventh hour became very critical. Especially as representatives of the Queen of England, the Oba of Benin, the Alafin of Oyo, the Oni of Ife, the Sultan of Sokoto,the Shehu of Bornu and other eminent traditional rulers were already seated. It was the first of such coronations to enjoy the benefits of modern mass communication - with the British Broadcasting Corporation, the Voice of America and the Ghana Broadcasting Corporation taking the coverage of the coronation live from Kumasi, Ghana.

In that critical hour, word passed round the Ashanti Royal Court of the emergency and it was the then traditional ruler of Sunyani, Nana Sarpong who suggested that Kwabena Donkor could be a perfect replacement. Kwabena's subsequent performance at the Coronation was the talk of a whole country gripped with the novelty of radio and the grandeur of the royal installation in the ancient Ashanti capital. He was subsequently elevated to the position of Linguist. But there was a snag. Given his vast trado – medical knowledge, and the need for his continuing proximity to the grove of his ancestral practice, his relocation to Kumasi was impossible. By the special grace of the Asentehene therefore, Kwabena remained in his village; and only performed his function as a Linguist only at very important Grade 'A' ceremonies, where his charisma and deep cultural savvy were required. He became therefore more than an ordinary orator; and went beyond the vague oratorical reputation to be recognized as the traditional medical consultant to the Royal Court and a renowned authority on the use of local herbs and necromancy. He often recited long spiritual incantations and had a large dosage of proverbs, puns and wise-cracks which usually earned him spontaneous applause. His deep-rooted proverbs often required deep reflections for their inner meanings to be deciphered. Despite his retentive memory

and his deep knowledge of history, events, the Ashanti culture and traditional healing methods, he was conscious of his main weakness. He
knew that he performed well and was appreciated because his age and
generation functioned at a verbal or oral level, with very little western
education or documentation.But he was wise to the fact that a genera-
tional shift to more western values that included writing and speaking
skills in the English language was fast developing. He therefore consciously exposed his children to western education so that they might
find a way of using modern western descriptions and botanical names
to document his traditional healing methods for posterity.

Abenaa, his first daughter had a special place in his heart. She was
born on a tuesday and was named Abenaa in line with Ashanti tradition
of naming children after the days of birth. Kwabena himself was born
on a tuesday and the fact that father and daughter not only shared the
same day of birth but also the same date of 31st of December reinforced
the warmth and bond between them. Abenaa was encouraged to go to
school; and provided with extra tutorials at home by the village's school
headmaster. Where the headmaster was busy, he delegated some of the
younger teachers to take charge as it was well known in the entire village that Nana Kwabena wanted the best for his daughter. It was hardly
surprising therefore that Abenaa passed in flying colours when she wrote
her primary school certificate exams.

She was an exceptionally brilliant girl and she quickly transferred her
ability to read and write to support the father's trado-medical practice.
Nana Kwabena doted over his daughter; and taught her skills that he
himself inherited from his fore-fathers. He would frequently take the
little girl into the forest to teach her the magic of nature; and the various
medical uses of herbs, the bark of trees and the stems of great plants.
The cherished Ashanti traditional medical heritage thus was gradually
documented as it was narrated and transferred from father to daughter.
Then suddenly, it was time for Abenaa to go to secondary school; and
only the best was good enough for her;and the best and the nearest girl's
secondary school being in Kumasi, she had to leave home for the first
time. Preparing for resumption at the school in Kumasi also coincided

with her traditional preparation for womanhood.

The Ashanti mother-child bond was traditionally strengthened by the matrilineal system of inheritance. The belief that the pure blood of the mother formed the child in the womb through the umbilical cord underlined the integrity of the mother-child relationship. There could be no doubt whatsoever about who your true mother was because of this biological covenant which the Ashantis called "magya". However, whilst the mother gave blood and biological life to the child, the Ashantis believed that the father breathe spiritual life into the child through the "sumsum". The initiation into womanhood demonstrated this social organization that supported the child's existence in an elaborate puberty rites that welcomed the girl into womanhood and the communal pronouncement of the girl's readiness for sexual expression strictly within the institution of marriage.

Preparations for Abenna's puberty rites reflected this social context. Her relationship with her father had always emphasised this spiritual bond. She had learnt the ways of her people, their culture, their habits and their medicines through the close bond with her father. But as the blood and biological source of the next generation of Ashantis, the very serious and complex rituals to cleanse and make her fertile for womanhood was one of the most important social functions in Ashanti society.

"What is this tree called… and how does it help our people… ? "

Father and daughter were in the Bechemtie jungle; as had become the pattern, almost a daily routine; as the transfer of trado-medical knowledge to Abenaa was a paramount consideration for Kwabena.

"Papa… I know this tree of course… is it not the "Nyankyerenee" tree ?… It has anti-bacteria, anti-viral and aromatic properties… You can use it for the treatment of boils, scabies, swellings… you can mix the droppings with clean water for the treatment of cataract…"

"Good… good girl… you know you will go to the white man's school… and you will be a doctor… you will combine the best of two great medical traditions… and you will be without a rival in the whole world…"

They both embraced with strong family bonding and continued in their search and tutorials. Nana Kwabena Donkor had a patient back in the village with symptoms he had diagnosed as pneumonia and gastritis; and was searching for the very rare wild versions of the "afema" tree and the root of the "mumunnini ahabam" tree. It was time for another round of tutorials when they finally found them. "... Naa," Kwabenna called her daughter fondly, whilst looking inquisitively into her eyes. "You see... these trees... they communicate... listen..." and he beckoned the eerie stillness of the jungle.

"... Did you hear anything?"

"No... Papa..."

"Don't worry... one day, very soon, you will be able to listen to the ways and extra – terrestrial communications of nature... one day. "

Then, he asked her to kneel down before the mighty tree and brought out of his bag, two eggs and a gourd of palm wine. He broke the eggs against the tree and sprinkled the palm wine in deep libation...

"Great 'afema' tree... I present you food and drink... I come in supplication for your sick son Oppong Kyekyeku. We have run to you in our hour of need... have mercy upon your son... release your treasured leaves, stems and barks for his treatment... so that he may be well again... Here... take this (pouring libation) offering from your son... He will be back to pay you homage once you have made him well again... Great 'afema'... I salute you..." Father and daughter rose up from their prayers in unison.

Kwabenna stepped forward to cut the bark of the tree. As he did so, he stumbled and hit his left toe against the stump of the undergrowth around the tree... and almost fell down...

"Abomination!!" he screamed

"Great Afema tree... my apologies... I hear you... Yes I will put my house in order and come back... Yes I will check the patient's antecedents... Yes perhaps he is being punished by the gods for an evil deed... Thank you... Thank you... We shall return"

"What was that all about?" Abenaa asked in childish innocence.

"I told you that one day... you would understand the various forms of communication of mother nature..." "So... what happened... Why are we not cutting the leaves again, Papa…"

"The afema tree has spoken… Somebody has defiled my compound… a sacrilege has occurred. Probably the patient had witchcraft… or one of my wives concealed her menstrual flow from me… and cooked for me… or slept with me… or one of my children… it could be anything and anyone. But the forest is angry… so I have to find out first before I return… But this is the period of "Afashe"… the festivals, the initiations and the puberty rites… I can only consult the oracle after the festivals and initiations… We will see then…"

That was one week ago. There were about fourteen girls who qualified for the puberty rites in the village that year. The only qualification being the recent commencement of "kyima" or menstrual flow bleeding. The fourteen girls had at different times seen the Queen Mother individually to confirm "three consecutive bleeding episodes" to qualify for the communal initiation rites. Abenaa's visit to the Queen Mother three consecutive months earlier had been without any incident. The Queen Mother had confirmed the "bleeding", checked that her hymen and virginity were intact, that her waist was fully developed for safe birth passage; her breasts were well-formed and pear-shaped with the nipples sharp, dark and protruding. Upon the Queen Mother's verdict of success at the pre – rites evaluation, Abenaa's proud mother had taken her to the village market for essential womanhood shopping… pants, brassieres, body creams, hair creams, gold ornaments and traditional "kente" cloth; coral beads, a special white stool, pillows and pillow cases, blanket, bed sheets, sleeping mats. From the house, Abenaa was supplied with cups, cooking pots and a mortar and pestle.

The Town Crier was out very early that morning to announce the beginning of the puberty rites for the fourteen girls. With an old gong and a whistle, he went round all four quarters of the village. At the Queen Mother's compound, the back garden prepared for the ceremonial ritual and stay of the girls played host to the highly expectant nubile beauties that morning. All of them naked, they took their first communal cold bath; accompanied by songs and chant by a band of supporting very elderly women. The young girls sang along, took few dance steps in unison as they took their communal baths.

Thereafter, they all filed back into the main compound to be anointed with white powder and mascara. When they next filed out, they were symbolically seated on white stools to symbolise purity. Each of the girls had a large basin of water in front of her into which was sprinkled perfumes and fresh leaves. They were now ready to have breakfast as a community of maidens. After breakfast, they were allowed to receive friends and family members who brought in gifts. All gifts by way of gold coins were thrown into the basin of water. That way, the content of individual basin was hidden from prying eyes to avoid unnecessary envy.

The next day, accompanied by exciting rhythms and nobility chants, Abenaa's maternal aunt, supported by friends and well wishers came over to the Queen Mother's to pay traditional homage to her little niece who was on the way to coming of age;and to perform the essential libation rites: As the most senior matrineal aunt, the role of pouring libation to the fore-fathers for Abenaa's safe transition into puberty was reserved for her. With a gourd of palm wine and a bottle of locally distilled gin - "akpeteshi,"- she liberally poured libation on the initiation grounds and prayed for good health, fertility and protection for her niece.

Midway into the week-long initiation ceremony, it was time for the traditional Ritual Bath. In preparation for the all-important ritual, Abenaa's hair, along with the other girls had been thoroughly shaved and cleansed with coconut oil. The shaved hair, her finger nails and toe nails were put in a calabash and handed over to the father for safe keeping; as these were believed to be essential DNA elements that must be guarded jealously by all Ashantis. For the purpose of the Ritual Bath, Abenaa and the other girls must not walk. Their feet must not touch the earth. So Abenaa was borne on the back of one of the older supporting women to the fast flowing Konongo River. A dance procession led the way and the music and singing continued as the Queen Mother ceremonially stripped her naked and gave her a rafia palm to cover with. A red piece of cloth was tied around her mid-section as the Queen Mother invoked the spirits with incantations as she immersed her in the fast flowing water for as long as her breath could hold her. As Abenaa came out of the water after the third immersion, the crowd of spectators roared in approval at the paragon of beauty, whose old childish ways had been spiritually washed away for a new life. Abenaa and the other girls returned to the village amid great drumming, singing and merriment. Led by the Queen Mother, the village's traditional female leader,they sang and invoked incantations and songs of praise all the way home....

"Where are you... I say.... where are you, all great men... Come and see prime Ashanti beauty... look closely at her robust, well-rounded provocative breast..."

This was followed by loud sighs of concurrence and applause.

"Look at her long – smooth legs... a beauty fit for a monarch's bed... to bear tall and beautiful Ashanti princes and princesses... Hurrah!! Can you see what I see... ? Her fleshy succulent buttocks... see how they bounce in locomotive rhythm... Hey... buttocks so soft that you will not require a mattress to support your love-making!"

And another round of excitement went through the crowd of onlookers and admirers. The on-lookers strained their necks to catch a glimpse of Abenna.

"Hello... hello... are you there... come, take a look at her pointed nose... and her succulent lips... hey! look at her eyes... romantic and seductive like the early morning dew and her tummy full of eggs... just waiting for the right Ashanti specimen of pure royal sperm... Hey! Come and see black luxuriant hair... with golden radiance."

The crowd of on-lookers roared in approval as they trooped along. Finally, the procession arrived at the Queen Mother's compound; where a great feast had been prepared. Mashed yam and plantain, blended into a marshy meal with eggs, palm oil and dry fish was then served in giant pots to the friends and well-wishers.

The next day was devoted to cleaning up. Abenaa, singing joyously took clothes and plates for washing. By evening, preparations were in high gear for the "graduation" ceremonies scheduled for the next day. The next day was a saturday; the long awaited day. Gaily dressed in all her new clothes, jewellery, shoes and special gold bangles, Abenaa proceeded on a processional house-to-house "thank you" tour of the village. Carried on her white stool and covered with a giant umbrella like a true "Queen Mother," Abenaa and her entourage moved round the village with a final stop-over at the Queen Mother's official residence for her final examination, approval and conclusion of the Puberty Rites.

That was when it happened. Abenaa had felt unwell all day. But she had passed it off as an aftermath of the hard work and the stress of the week-long encampment. All through the thank you tour, she had barely managed to suppress a choking feeling of nausea. But as she was brought down and lowered into the presence of the Queen Mother in her inner chamber, she was suddenly overcome by the urge to vomit. Try as she did, she could not hold it back as she threw up vomit all over the Queen Mother's inner chamber.

"Bring water, someone... get her water to drink... clean the floor... common..." The Queen Mother instructed.

With the floor and Abenaa now cleaned up; the Queen Mother turned what she had planned to be a joyous perfunctory inspection and approval into a more serious task. She invited Abenaa to lie down; and with her experienced fingers,she clinically examined her eyes; her nipples and her hymen! Next, she felt the ovarian passage and the womb.

"Abomination!" The Queen Mother screamed, as an oppressive silence descended on the inner chamber. In very hush-hush tones, the message was passed around. Summon Nana Kwabenna Donkor immediately. The unspeakable had happened. The pride of the village. Nana Kwabenna's blue-eyed girl was not only guilty of pre puberty-rites and pre-marital sexual intercourse, she was pregnant!!

A panting Nana Kwabena arrived the Queen Mother's residence in a state of frenzy and anxiety. Before her distraught father, Abenaa confessed to having been pounced upon in her sleep and raped by one of the young village teachers! That true, she never realized she was pregnant until...

So this was the reason, Nana thought. "Oh" he sighed, realizing that the jungle had communicated the abomination in his household much earlier. But for the "Afashe" festival and the ban on divination during the period, he would have unravelled this before now. And could have avoided this community-wide disgrace.

"Nyame!" Nana Kwabenna screamed, shaking his hands, legs and head violently in anger

"Hey!"

That night, the guilty teacher was summoned. It was a very short trial, as there was no denial of the sacrilege by both parties. The sentencing panel was made up of the Queen Mother and Nana Kwabenna himself. The offence committed was a grievous one indeed. It was an offence that could bring retribution not just upon the village; but against the entire Ashanti Kingdom. Ashanti land and its gods had been defiled. A heinous crime of "kyiribra" had been committed. The Great Forest had spoken to Nana Kwabenna much earlier: Clean up your sacrilege or don't return. The medical needs of the Ashanti nation would not be serviced by the Great Forest until... The repercussions of "kyiribra" were well-known: Prolonged droughts, famine, pestilence, premature births, deformities and wild forest fires had been known to visit defiant guilty communities; or communities who had made fraudulent attempts to conceal the abomination.

"Hey... Naa!" Nana Kwabenna screamed, gazing at her daughter with blood-shot eyes. But his penetrating gaze went beyond her. He was thinking more of the ritual bath on the fast-flowing Konongo River; and how this "kyribra" occurrence had polluted the only source of fish and fresh water to the community.

Early the next morning, the great task of purifying the land commenced. Kwabenna and the Queen Mother having considered all the issues related to the abomination had come to a unanimous conclusion and the very painful verdict: purification and exile! That morning, teacher Osei Owusu and Abenaa Donkor were stripped naked and paraded through the four corners of Nsesereso. Curses and sand were rained on them as they were paraded and flogged with plantain leaves. They were led out of the town, deep into the edge of the Great Forest. There, a sacrificial ram was held high and slaughtered over the heads of the guilty couple who had polluted the land. As the blood trickled down their bodies, the elders watched with interest to observe the direction of the trickle. Finally, the blood trickled into the genitals of Abenaa and Osei to signify the acceptance of the sacrifice by the gods, and the crowd roared in relief; as they knew that the goat's blood in their genitalia was a sign that their purification and sacrifice had been accepted by the gods. Thereafter, Abenaa and Osei were flogged and exiled into the Great Forest, never to return to Ashanti land.

She could never explain where the courage came from. But she had been brought up to be proud, confident and independent. The father's "sumsum" lived in her and she embodied his knowledge. So she could understand the father's anger and commitment to traditional justice. She, Abenaa had brought shame and disappointment to her father. Her father, a custodian of culture and tradition, the voice and conscience of the fore-fathers in the revered ancient Ashanti Royal Court. To be seen bending the rules and obstructing the course of traditional justice? No, so, she understood. Perfectly.

As she walked deeper and deeper into the Great Forest, she felt nothing but anger and revulsion at the source of her disgrace and predicament. Osei! Sneaky... shifty... crafty and fraudulent wimp! That would abuse the trust and innocence of an adolescent! The gods would truly judge him, she cursed as she walked confidently down the bush path and deeper into the forest. She was in a familiar terrain as she quickly adopted a north-easterly direction towards an abandoned hunter's farm house that she had come across in the past.

"Abenaa... Abenaa... please wait for me..." It was the shrill voice of Osel, the teacher, as he struggled to catch up with the firm strides of Abenaa.. "... You fool... how dare you!"

"Please, forgive me... I never meant any harm... It must have been the work of the devil... I truly love you... please forgive me..."

Surely, Osei must have been in league with the devil himself, Abenaa thought, as she reflected on the source and cause of her current misery. Three months into his transfer to Nsesereso from the Techiman Native Authority School, he had assumed a notoriety with the pupils as a wimp who covered up for his weaknesses with the whip. Armed with a strong,long rafia palm cane, he would come to class ready to flog and assault his pupils at every excuse. In a very short while, he had become a monster in the erstwhile sleepy one-block village school. It did not take long for Osei to realize that the most pretty female pupil in the school also happened to be the most intelligent and the daughter of the most successful man in Nsesereso. But too shy to make a direct approach, he soon resorted to threats and intimidation to get close to Abenaa. "

"Hey you... yes... you come with me to the Staff Room" Young, innocent Abenaa will oblige dutifully. But the docile pupil received no respite. "Yes... carry my books and my cane to the house"

Abenaa would carry the books on her head and would be instructed to walk in front of teacher Osei. Osei's pleasures knew no limits as he walked daily behind the well-formed and provocative buttocks of Abenaa as they bounced in steady rhythm to her graceful steps. Osei's penetrating gaze would undress the innocent girl's behind all the way to his house, where reluctantly, but authoritatively, he would dismiss the very pliable innocent girl.

More and more, his fantasies and wet dreams were occupied by the looming image of Abenaa. He found himself looking more and more towards the occasional opportunity provided by the absence of the headmaster to give Abenaa private lessons at home. Those opportunities to be all alone with the girl to steal a glance at her ripening breast and make the occasional "accidental" body contact fuelled Osei's passion and occupied his nights.

At school, the one block mud building that served as the community school had a pit latrine at the end of it. Next to the pit latrine was the Staff Room. Osei had cleverly drill a hole between the wall of the Staff Room and the latrine; and there he feasted his eyes every day with the sights of young female genitalia anytime they used the toilet.

In another age with proper communication and administrative records, Osei's child molestation and paedophilic antics would have been of common knowledge to the security agencies. It would have been clear to the old, soon to retire headmaster of the Nserereso community school that the new young teacher, recently transferred from Techiman was not to be trusted with female children. But the transfer letter was general in nature: Transferred on grounds of discipline; which Osei had glibly explained off as disagreements with the authorities in his former school in Techiman. There, Osei had been caught cliinging to the roof members in the open ceiling of a toilet adjacent to the female toilet feasting his eyes and passions on young naked female pupils.

When, upon his resumption in Nsesereso, the headmaster had asked him to fill in for him occasionally at Nana Kwabenna Donkor's residence, he could hardly disguise his secret joy at the opportunity to be one-on-one with Abenaa from time to time.

Three months earlier, the week had started on an eventful note for Abenaa. She woke up that sunday morning to find herself drenched in blood. She found that the bed was similarly drenched and she panicked. She checked for the source of the injury and traced it to her thighs. She was gripped with fear. The bond between father and daughter was manifested when in her hour of distress, Abenaa rushed out of the room, complete with all the blood stains and rushed to the father's shrine at the rear of a grove in the compound.

"Nana... I am dying..." she managed to utter, when the father stopped her at the entrance to his shrine. "Stop there... Stop this very minute... Stop. Do you want to defile this shrine? Stop right there..." This was a different view of the ever-loving and... doting father that she knew."

"Papa..."

"Shut up! I know... what you want to say... don't even utter it...."

"Akosua... Akosua... Akosua" Nana Kwabenna shouted down the grove; to summon Abenaa's mother, who came running down...

"You see your carelessness... ? what kind of mother are you? Are you a woman at all? That you cannot educate your only daughter on the simple rules of nature... That you are not even observant enough to know that this day was near... and to prepare your daughter for it... careless woman! Take your daughter away from here before the gods get angry with you... careless woman!"

That sunday, her mother Akosua had spent the whole day explaining the various stages in the life of a woman. She had explained the menstrual cycle, the "monthly bleeding" and the other changes in her breasts and mammary glands. But Abenaa could never overcome the anxiety of losing so much blood. Psychologically, she saw the blood coming out of her body as a drain on her source of vitality; and was resultantly drained physically during and after her now traditional four-day "bleeding". But she felt weak nevertheless any time she had to go through the bleeding spell. So when on that saturday afternoon about three months after her first bleeding and one week after her third bleeding, teacher Osei had come knocking for her regular lessons, she was tired and in deep slumber. Osei had knocked at the door of the main house without response. He knew Nana Kwabenna Donkor would be busy down at the shrine in the grove far away, so he went over to the wife's hut and knocked: No reply. He pushed the door slightly and it slid open to present a heavenly sight. The sight of the subject of his dreams and fantasies... almost naked with just a small loin cloth on her chest spread-eagled in deep sleep. He tapped her breast to wake her up... but she stretched even more provocatively and continued her sleep. Quickly, Osei went down on his knees and started fondling her clitoris and put her firm nipples in his month... fondling and sucking rhythmically... Osei was now lost in the wilderness between Abenaa's clitoris and her breast.... Abenaa was now wet all over from the fondling... Quickly, Osei pulled off the buttons of his knickers and his erect penis burst through the narrow opening. He did not have to think... he did not even think or bother about pulling off his knickers... His actions were now spontaneous... on some programmed auto-pilot. With one swift and deft move, he mounted and simultaneously penetrated the sleeping Abenaa. The sharp pain woke Abenaa up... and a frantic spontaneous cry escaped her lips, as she opened her eyes to see the strange weight of teacher Osei on top of her. She struggled timidly and in fear, conscious of the teacher and pupil relationship, and teacher Osei's reputation with the rafia cane.

She half cried with muffled shouts and subdued grunts as teacher Osei pounded and inflicted more pains. Then finally Osei stretched and jerked nervously... slowly at first... and more forcefully without control as he crashed into a sudden stillness on top of her.

Quickly he got up and buttoned his stained knickers. Seeing that his knickers had been strained with blood and semen, he brought down his shirt and flew it over the knickers... and in very low tones...

"It is good... God created man and woman to do this always... it will get better and better between us... and don't mention this to anybody... Never!" He was now standing and clutching his raffia cane.

"Never mention this to anybody... it must be kept secret... just the two of us... a secret we share..." Abenaa hissed in disdain. It was over so quickly... and it was so so painful. Not the fantasies and pleasures that her mother had talked about three months earlier.

Abenaa walked deeper into the Great Forest. She by-passed the farming settlements of Dorma, Ahenkro and Atuma. By nightfall, she located the abandoned hunters' hut; a hut previously used by farmers from the village of Banne during the last hunting expedition. There, she helped herself with some condemned clothes from an old sack with which she made a wrap-around skirt and a rough blouse. From another sack, she made a blanket and a loose cloth to cover with during the cold night. She was not hungry. Just angry; as she thought through her plight throughout the sleepless night. The next morning, she commenced efforts to make the hut more habitable. She collected palm fronds for the roof and side walls and located a steam nearby. She explored further and found wild berries and cherry fruits. She collected enough and returned to the hut. That evening, she embarked on her most important challenge. All through the night, her sleep had been troubled with fleeting images of a crying baby and her doting father's herbal teachings and admonition. As dawn broke, her father's image loomed larger in his caring voice.

"... Abenaa, my daughter... this one... yes, this plant is very dangerous... No pregnant woman must chew the leaves or stem... it induces spontaneous abortion and uterine bleeding... experienced physicians use it to regulate irregular menstrual cycles..."

Abenaa searched the Great Forest until she found what she was looking for:the great "ayamtum "fertility tree; with leaves so broad that the leaf was worn as a cap to symbolize fertility at every Queen Mother's initiation. The pungent smell from the bark so strong that it repelled insects, rodents and reptiles. With her bare hands, Abenaa climbed into the tree trunk and plucked a few leaves. Then she prayed for forgiveness to the mighty tree and cut a small portion from the bark. On her way back to the hut, she collected some "toantini" leaves and fresh palm nut fruits. Later; she put all she had collected to boil and left the mixture to ferment for seven days. She started drinking the mixture freely from the eighth day and the result was instantaneous: Nausea, vomiting and vaginal bleeding. This was followed by excruciating stomach pains the next day. In all her pains, every attempt by Osei, who had by now smuggled himself into the hut to offer assistance was rebuffed sharply. By the third day, the bleeding had gradually stopped and the pains had eased off. That day, Abenaa feasted herself on fresh wild fruits and a lot of water. She did this for the next one week as she felt her strength return gradually.

With her strength back, she set about looking for a source of protein for her meals. She tried bare hand and pond fishing by the stream, but was unsuccessful. Then she chanced upon the "ahodjo" plant:stunted and sinewy. Very strong recoil when bent and a trapper's best friend. She prepared three stems of the "ahodjo" plant with some metal strings that she saw in the hut as traps and put the appropriate bait. Her joy knew no bonds when one of the traps caught an antelope the next morning. With her food and shelter now taken care of, Abenaa settled down to explore the Great Forest fully. She was away for two days of exploration where she discovered numerous settlements and villages. In one of the villages, she over heard people speak a language that was close to her Ashanti dialect. She also established that the village had a market which met every four days. She made plans to take some of the fruits and wild animals she trapped to the market. But first, out of pity and expression of her trado-medical gift, she had to attend to Osei and his nagging ailment.

For over a week, Osei had moaned and grunted repeatedly about a stomach ache. It started with constipation after eating wild berries and cherries. Osei's system had been unable to expel the resultant waste. Osei's body had been exposed to decaying waste material and opportunistic infections. Abenaa had ignored all his cries for help before now; but as the illness got progressively worse, with signs of peptic ulcer and flatulence, she had reluctantly decided to help. That afternoon, she prepared a wild aloe-vera paste and boiled the fresh leaves of wild "bosontwe" and administered same on Osei. Four days later, he was well again.

Abenaa's two-day walk through the Great Forest in a south-westerly direction had taken her across the unmarked borders of Ivory Coast and to her new abode. Without realizing that she was in Ivory Coast, she had pitched her new settlement with locational proximity to her daily needs –food,water,shelter and security. Conveniently located on a tributary of the Bayakokore River, her first trip to the market near Tanda was very profitable. She sold wild cherry, some pears and two antelopes. With the money realized, she bought some clothes and a pair of slippers. She also bought household items like pot, oil, salt, pepper, onions and tomatoes.

Without realizing it, the border point between Ghana and Ivory Coast where Abenaa crossed had always been part of one continuous Akan community until the colonial partitionists and surveyors drew arbitrary lines of demarcation between the two countries. The Agni and Baoule people of Ivory Coast, victims of internecine and leadership tussles in the old Ashanti empire had had their settlements pillaged and forced into migration into modern day Ivory Coast.They kept the essential traditions of the old Ashanti empire and continued to speak a dialect of Akan language, as Abenaa was to find out later. The use of the symbolic lineage stool named after the founding female of the lineage and their matrilineal social organisational structures were retained and continued to reflect their Ashanti antecedents. Abenaa was therefore quite comfortable with her limited interaction and communication during market days.

She did not hear the announcement the first time. But when the market crier came round the second time, he was slower and more deliberate:The municipal council in Tanda urgently required auxiliary nursing assistants. Although, a first school leaving certificate was required, those without the qualification should apply all the same for training.

At the recruitment centre set up by the council near the market, she was interviewed and accepted for training. Abenaa never returned to the bush settlement; for the offer provided a unique opportunity to erase the pathetic Osei from her life and her memory. The auxiliary nursing assistant training was rudimentary. The role was essentially the provision of menial support to the staff nurses. Cleaning and disinfecting the wards, washing and ironing of beddings, scrubbing of the toilets, washing of the walls and washing and ironing of the nurse's uniforms. But the real reason the job was unattractive to a level that the municipal council had to canvass for volunteers in the market place was the cleaning of patients' faeces and urine; the washing of fresh corpses before transfer to the mortuary; and the washing of blood-stained and infected beddings. But most importantly, the position provided free accommodation within the premises of the hospital.

The new job provided a good break for Abenaa who took upon the task with gusto. The offer provided a squalid living dormitory at the rear of the hospital and feeding from the central kitchen. The little she earned, she spent for her French language lessons and correspondence courses. She learnt quickly and could speak and write French fairly well at the end of two years. Through observation, she had taught herself basic medical nursing. She could administer drugs, inject patients, and take blood pressure and pulse. She could bandage, apply dressings so well that she attracted the attention of the Medicin Sans Frontiere (MSF) volunteer Doctor Phil Home, who was on a short-term attachment to the hospital.

Six months into her stay, Doctor Phil Home was transferred to the MSF – run hospital in Gbegamey – Nord in Abidjan. She had come to like the quiet and dependable disposition of Abenaa and convinced the hard working nursing mate to move to Abidjan with her. Abenaa accepted with concealed joy, happy at the opportunity to move to the big city she had heard so much about.

It was a very big hospital, with facilities for major surgical operations. Abenaa was assigned to the male surgical ward as Nursing Assistant. Gone were the menial scrubbing and washing jobs. She was also given new blue uniforms to reflect her new status. Her duties included the documentation of patient's vital statistics, administration of drugs, cleaning of patients and liaison with the kitchen for patients' meals. At home in the Cocody area very near the hospital where she lived with her MSF doctor friend, she assisted Doctor Home with house cleaning and cooking chores.

Abidjan was a beautiful town. The outcast girl from Nsesereso, the sleepy village of just over a hundred huts saw rows and rows of high rise buildings. The cars! She lost her breath counting the number of cars on the streets of Abidjan! Back in the village in Nesesereso, the only car that came to the village was the Asantehene's car; and that only for very important royal functions when the services of Kwabenna Donkor were required. Doctor Home took her on a drive on the MSF Peugeot pick-up van around Abidjan that first weekend: They drove through Williams Ville all the way to the zoo. They returned through Adjame to the other end of town around the Embassy area and Tresils Ville.

Three months into their stay in Abidjan, they were at a supermarket on a Saturday afternoon shopping at the Plateau area when the hospital Runner rushed into the parking lot on his Mobylette bike, looking frantic. He passed a note to Doctor Home, which ended their jolly ride and shopping as a major surgical emergency had arisen in the hospital.

When they got to the hospital, two mud-splattered and discoloured MSF ambulances were parked at the entrance with rotating strobe lights. The accompanying MSF doctor took Doctor Home aside to brief her of the situation. Abenaa was to later piece all of the information together: Following the outbreak of hostilities between Area Fada's insurgent rebel army and the Armed Forces of Liberia, casualties with severe gun-shot wounds had been pouring across the border into the MSF hospital in San Pedro. The pressure on San Pedro was such that it then required more surgical supplies and more surgical hands. The ambulances had already been loaded with supplies, but could Doctor

Home be kind enough to travel with the party to give a helping hand? A quick consultation between Doctor Home and Abenaa led to a drive home and hurried packing.

They drove through the night, arriving San Pedro just before dawn. San Pedro, though in Ivory Coast and not part of the civil war in Liberia was like a theatre of battle. Scores and scores of military vehicles loaded with supplies. Soldiers in uniforms.

Soldiers in mufti. Some, even younger than Abenaa and all looking dazed and weary from battle fatigue. The hospital was a small cottage affair. The injured were spread beyond the wards into all the adjoining grass lawns and verandah. Cries of pain and deadly grunts as the wounded writhed in pains. The heavy odour of decaying flesh, the putrid smell of gangrene mingled with anti-biotic and carbolic was over-whelming.

Doctor Home and Abenaa settled into the field tent assigned to them and tried to get some sleep after the overnight travel. Two narrow camp beds and a plastic hanger were the only item of furniture in the tent. Abenaa collapsed the camp bed, flattened into a blanket and quickly fell asleep. She had lived off the land before and was very much at home in her new environment.

The Ward Round started the next morning with Doctor Home. Sharpnel extractions, burns, bullet wounds, amputations, fractures, dislocations, shell-shock, temporary insanity, the list was endless. So were the number of patients stretched along corridors and the lawns. The more senior combatants were accommodated in field tents on the open lawns. In one of those tents there was a heightened security cordon with heavily armed combatants providing perimeter security. When Doctor Home and Abenaa stepped into the high security tent, they found a disheveled man in delirium.

"Whh! Ehh! Shoot me! Kill me! Let me die... Can't bear this suffering any longer... Shoot me... I say shoot me now"

The case file revealed multiple gun shot wounds to the chest and abdomen and explosive ordnance damage to the two lower limbs. The patient was still in shock and needed immediate surgery. Given the lack of theatre space, Doctor Home made an immediate decision to operate in the tent. Armed with her field surgical case and a battery-operated surgical theatre lighting, she set to work immediately with Abenaa as Theater Assistant. For sterilization, water was put to boil on a charcoal fire just outside the tent. It was a four-hour operation that patched the punctured gut, the thoracic membrane and the left upper abdominal region. The fractured lower limbs were treated and dressed conservatively to avoid infection and to await a major orthopaedic surgery some other day. Doctor Home could hear a hushed anxiety and excitement outside as she completed the post-operative documentation inside the tent: Name of patient: Abu Mondei. Age – 35, Sex – Male, Nationality – Sierra Leonian, Occupation – Captain, RUf Detachment, National Patriotic Front (NPFL). Combatant.

This combatant, evacuated from the theatre of conflict in Liberia across the border was admitted with multiple gun shot injuries and fracture to his lower limbs as a result of bomb explosion.... Emergency surgical procedure to extract bullet lodged in scapula... and to patch punctured thoracic membrane and his alimentary canal was successful. Patient remains in very critical stage... still in coma... damage to lower limbs treated for infection... recommended for major orthopaedic procedure...

"Doctor! Ehen Doctor... how is my boy... okay?" A burly looking, bearded man with bold, blood-shot eyes and a swagger stick, asked as he parted the curtains and entered the tent.

"Please... could you wait outside... this is a surgical theatre... please outside... you may infect the patient..."

"Me! Infect my boy... Doctor, listen that boy must not die... do all you can... okay let's go outside..." The man led Doctor Home outside the tent and she could see a whole new detachment of combat-ready body guards and young girls in tight – fitting jeans trousers and jackets armed to the teeth with AK 47s and RPGs.

"... Yes Doctor... my name is Corporal Foday Sankoh... RUF..." he volunteered his identity once they were outside the tent.

"... Papay... Papei... Papa Morlai" the crowd of combatants hailed him in riotous spontaneity. When he lifted his hands, there was absolute silence as he walked the Doctor to his command jeep whilst being briefed on the overall state of health and prognosis of Captain Mondei. Doctor Home bid him farewell as his motorcade left in a riot, with needless salvos of gunshots fired into the air. She and Abenaa performed seven other surgical operations that day. They retired exhausted, went for their first meal of the day and slept off, even whilst still eating.

"Why are you fighting in Liberia when you are a Sierra Leonian?" Abenna asked Captain Mondei, one morning, a full month after his initial surgery. As the Captain recovered, she had come to associate a sharp intellect with him. His sense of humour and intelligent wit despite his pains was amazing.

"Why are you nursing people in Ivory Coast, when you are a Ghanaian?" captain Mondei retorted. Abenaa was shocked. No one, not even Doctor Home knew her inner secrets and her Ghanaian origins... so how did Captain Modei find out?. She suddenly burst out in cold sweat... and replied nervously...

"Who told you I am a Ghanaian?"

"I know... it is my duty to know... come, sit down here" asking her to sit on a nearby chair.

"No! I won't! Why do you make these false statements?"

"What statement? That you are Ghanaian... what's wrong with being a Ghanaian? You should be proud... very proud"

She made to retort... but was unable. She kept quiet and allowed him to continue.

"Abenaa..." the captain continued.

The shock hit her and it showed on her face. She had been "Sister Tessy" since her menial auxiliary nursing days in Tanda... and all her MSF records carried that name and an Ivorian nationality.

"You see you don't understand. My field of specialization in the army is military intelligence. Doctor Home is French of course, but has a

Belgian mother and has an elder brother in the French Foreign Legion. You are originally Ghanaian… an Ashanti obviously… now claiming Ivorian nationality… a very gifted and well respected medical nursing assistant by the MSF… did you know that your friend Doctor Home is being recalled to France?" This time, Abenaa could not disguise her shock, she broke out in sweat nervously… made to swallow… but her throat and lips went dry suddenly.

"Yes… the brother is an early fatality in a bold reconnaissance operation in Iraq…"

"But the war has not started… the Geneva Peace Talks…"

"My Dear… the most important battle in any war is the pre-battle before the out-break of hostilities… that is when the eventual war is won and lost… Your friend's brother was infiltrated into Iraq for some covert operation… he was shot during extraction… The father has been informed… the mother is divorced, now resident in Belgium… so that's why Doctor Home is being recalled… she is quite close to the father you know…" Abenaa did not know that and her shock showed it.

Infact, Abenna knew very little about Doctor Home beyond their professional relationship.

"So how do you know these things?"

"Common, you think I will entrust my life to people I don't know… Since I regained consciousness, I have been commissioning and receiving daily intelligence mission reports." Abenaa was shocked. How could Doctor Home conceal so much from her… and to think that they share the same tent! Without uttering a word, she stormed out of Captain Mondei's tent, with her head and shoulders held high in indignation. Doctor Home was fast asleep when Abenaa returned to their living quarters. Abenaa sat up, waiting for the doctor to wake up so she could get an explanation on what she had just heard from Captain Mondei.

But the whole day passed without incident as Doctor Home went about her normal duties. She was her usual self that night, played her jazz music and updated her African diary. Abenaa was confused. She could not confront the doctor with what she had heard for fear of raising a false alarm. What if Captain Mondei was wrong, she reasoned. She decided to shelve the discussion, sleep over the problem and possibly discuss it the next day. The next morning, they had a quick breakfast together and commenced their normal ward round. They were in the main male surgical ward, when the Medical Director beckoned to Doctor Home to join him in his office. She came out of the Medical Director's office beaming with smiles. She confided in Abenaa that she had been nominated to attend a donors' conference in Paris; and would have to leave for Abidjan immediately to catch an Air France flight the next day.

The real reason for Doctor Home's trip to Paris only dawned on Abenaa when she slept alone in the tent that night. Her sleep was troubled and she had repeated nightmares… Doctor Home unveiling an epitaph in slow motion in a large cemetery… Doctor Home at a funeral mass reading the first lesson… Doctor Home laying a wreath… Abenaa woke up sweating. God! It was all a ploy to get her back to Paris!!!. Her friend and benefactor had been taken away from her; and she did not even have an opportunity to say good- bye. How cruel! God! So Captain Mondei was right afterall! Abenaa wept throughout the night: Her thoughts went back to the chance encounter with Doctor Home at the Tanda rehabilitation project and how she impressed at the capacity building and health training programme run by the MSF.

Doctor Home had explained the core values of the organization. The provision of humanitarian assistance and in raising awareness of crisis situations, vaccination programmes and how as witnesses to the voiceless, the organization's personnel had often been exposed at the centre of crisis world-wide. That in the MSF's bid to alleviate human suffering, protect life and ensure respect for human dignity and fundamental human rights, the organization's personnel took grave personal risks. These grave risks lead to collateral casualties in the so many theatres of war where away from the glamour of the international media, the MSF toils with dignity to alleviate human suffering and bring hope to the hopeless. Doctor Home explained that anyone including Abenaa could become a local volunteer. Not for the money, because you only get a stipend, but to commit to the ideals of the organization. But it took time with interviews by the HR people, introductory courses, the endless stand-by status and the call to serve. Home explained that her field mission was for an initial period of six months, which she intended to extend by another six months. That Abenaa could work for her as a nursing assistant in any of her mission areas as a local aide without being on the direct employment and payroll of the organization.

Abenaa had gladly accepted the offer. As she thought over the events that morning, she could hardly hold back her tears. But on a second thought, she steeled herself and rose up in dignity. She had been through more difficult times, she thought. Having been together with Doctor Home for about eight months, her current mission duration would have ended in another month anyway. There and then, she resolved to commit her life to the ideals of the organization, even if she had to work outside of it. Afterall, she thought, if the likes of Doctor Home could travel from distant places to Africa to offer humanitarian assistance, what about her,an African.. why can't she provide that succour to fellow Africans? With or without an organization to support her, Abenaa decided to go ahead with her current efforts and commit her future to humanitarian work.

The atmosphere around Captain Mondei's tent was unusually quiet and sombre that friday morning. The previous day, Abenaa had been introduced to the replacement volunteer surgeon who took over from Doctor Home. A tall, chain- smoking and very brusque American, he had made it very clear that Abenaa could stay on as volunteer nursing assistant for as long as she wanted. Being a male had of course created difficulties with the accommodation and Abenaa had had to be relocated to a smaller tent near the field kitchen. Assured of her continuing role, she had come visiting in very high spirits when she was confronted with the sombre mood around the tent.

"How is my patient doing today?" She asked as she parted the curtains and entered the tent. There was no reply. Instead, she saw an unimaginable side to the usually self-assured Captain Mondei. Captain Mondei in tears! The sobs and grunts were so loud that they were overheard by the security aides outside, hence their sober mood.

Abenaa went out to the fire-place outside and the sterilizing cauldron and came back with hot water in a bowl. She soaked a clean towel in the hot water and gently, methodically started cleaning up the captain. She started with the face... wiped off his tears... moved to the hands... then the hairy chest... his tummy and groin. As she cleaned and massaged the captain methodically, a warm, erotic sensation filled him... He was filled with longing as he swallowed saliva repeatedly in eager lust. She turned him around and continued with the massage... started with his sore neck, progressing gradually down to his bare buttocks and inner thighs. With the hot towel between his things and her stroking fingers caressing his spinal chord, captain Mondei wished for no other heaven. He ejaculated involuntarily...

Exhausted, he fell asleep... his worries and anxieties banished for the time being. Abenaa sat by the bedside for a while, in deep thoughts analyzing the powers of alternative therapies. Where she could have given Captain Mondei a shot each of tradyl and ultragene, she had managed to achieve the same results without the side effects of those drugs through natural stimulation of the body's sensory mechanisms. It was a valuable lesson, because she had often wondered why modern medical practice often ignored, often looked upon traditional healing methods with suspicion. If science is supposed to be open-minded, transparent and pragmatic, the fixation to the "one and only route" approach by orthodox medical practitioners can never extend the frontiers of human knowledge, she thought.

There was a celebration party that evening on the lawns outside the Medical Director's office. It was a quiet celebration. But by the very quiet standards of the organization, it was comparatively loud. The Medical Director had announced that it was a double celebration as the organization had won two awards. The first one was the "Prix de la Concorde" which was awarded to the organization by the Principe de Astoria in May of that year for exemplary contribution to World Peace and Humanity and the Medal of Peace received at the 29th International Folklore Festival of Lefkas for the organization's courage, selflessness and dedication to the humanitarian needs of the less privileged and inaccessible, strife-torn communities world-wide. There were drinks, small chops and a speech by the Medical Director. He thanked all the volunteers, reminding them that it was through the cumulative efforts of people like them spread through the theatres of crisis, disease and deprivation all around the world that these awards had been achieved. He reminded all that the World was watching and would never forget their good deeds. With lively banters, discussions and drinks, the party dragged on till midnight.

Abenaa was just about to leave the party when three scruffy looking soldiers accosted her. The soldiers introduced themselves as Captain Mondei's body guards and that the captain was in severe pains and had requested for the attention of "Sister Tessy". Abenaa wondered what was so serious that the Captain would breach protocol to ask for her services personally.

The atmosphere in Captain Mondei's tent was shocking. The Captain had managed to prop himself up on bed, supported by pillows and was shedding profuse tears. His wailing and curses in his native Creole language cast a sombre mood around the tent. His case file usually tagged on the foot of his bed had been detached and he was leafing through it in uncontrollable tears. As he saw Abenaa, he flung the case file into the air cursing.

"… E beta le I die… to cut me foot… le' I no waka no more…… unu lie!... I say nurse…… unu lie… le' I die!! Let me die… kill me one tem… one tem… kill me at once… let me die… !!"

Abenaa did her best to calm him down, as she picked up the case file and read through it. Then she saw it.

The Consultant Orthopaedic Surgeon from Abidjan had finally arrived and after a few more x-rays and clinical examinations had concluded that the lower limb infections were getting gangrenous with severe risk of septicaemia. To save the captain's life therefore, the surgeon had recommended an immediate surgical operation to amputate the two lower limbs. The operation was scheduled for the next morning!

As Abenaa read through the note of finality in the surgeon's diagnosis, treatment plan and prognosis, even she a professional nurse could not hold back her tears. Spontaneously, they both broke into tears as she looked deeply into the sorrow of his eyes. Such intellect! Such brilliance!! Such a handsome, tall well-built man!!! What a loss!!! These were the thoughts running through Abenaa's mind as she shed uncontrollable tears. She could not explain it. At the height of her misery in her darkest hour at Nsesereso, she had held her head high with dignity... even then, she was much younger. But to now shed tears for the plight of a combatant who was a chance acquaintance and his patient for that matter. It was a very unprofessional conduct, she thought as she quickly got up to correct herself. Instantly, she changed her demeanor and carriage, assuming a professional bearing once again.

"Well... this is for your own good... to save your life... the surgeon has recommended post-operative physiotherapy and prosthetics... and I am sure it will be alright" Abenaa consoled the Captain professionally.

"But... not to ever walk again?..."

"No... who said ?... With proper physiotherapy and prosthetics, you can walk with the aid of clutches and..."

"Stop it... you are hurting me with your consolations... I don't need your sympathy... I would rather die"

"No. You will not die..." There was absolute silence in the tent, as Abenaa thought through her various options. Finally, she calmed the Captain and asked for some time.

"I am not promising anything... but I will see what I can do. Let me think about what to do and revert back to you later this night... I am sure there must be something we can do... Let's see how it goes... See you later then"

With that, Abenaa walked out of the tent into the dark night leaving a happier Captain Mondei behind. She went through a laboured night; troubled by the implications of the various options available to her. But early that morning, she came back to her earlier inner convictions: To serve humanity with all her might and with all her God-given talent. After that she felt at peace with herself.

When Captain Mondei saw the tools of the orthopaedic surgeon's trade, he was even more convinced about the wisdom of his decision. He had been thoroughly scrubbed and shaved that morning in preparation for his surgery. His pulse and blood pressure readings were surprisingly normal. He was a man who was beyond caring about this and the world of the surgeon at that point. He had refused to donate his blood for possible re-transfusion during the surgery because he insisted he would not need it. He looked around the operating theater again and was shocked at the ugliness of the orthopaedic surgical instruments. There were all kinds and sizes of saws arranged on a white table cloth in ascending order of ugliness and awe. The next table had an array of knives, cutlasses and a short menacing axe. At the centre was the biggest syringe he had ever seen. The Doctor walked in briskly, very business-like as the head of a team that included an anaesthetist, a surgical assistant and Abenaa as nursing assistant.

"How are you this morning?",the surgeon drawled. Without waiting for a response from Captain Mondei, the surgeon continued. "You will be fine... it is a very straight – forward procedure... we will take the limbs off just above your knee, stem the blood flow into the lower limb area... all of these will happen after we put you to sleep so you won't have to worry about anything... we will give you a small shot to relax you... Doctor Beckley here is your anaesthetist... Doctor Ingermann will be assisting me during the surgery and sister Tessy... your nurse...

"Good. Now that we are through with the introductions... If you will just sign this little slip for me... so that we can proceed..." as he handed Captain Mondei a small carbonized form.

For what looked like eternity, Captain Mondei studied the form. He adjusted the bed to have an upright position; surveyed the theatre and looked straight into the surgeon's eyes...

"Doctor... this is all so scary! All of these instruments of torture, cutlasses, saws, axes... is there no alternative to these brutal tools? I feel like I am in an abattoir... or probably a butcher's shed... There must be an alternative to this butchery procedure... and I want that alternative!"

The surgeon recovered first and retorted sarcastically. "Officer... you are entitled to your opinion about our surgical instruments... but honestly, I don't think you have a choice... The infection from your lower limbs is already over-powering all the anti-biotic we have administered so far.... And infecting your blood stream... if we don't take the legs off now... you don't stand a chance... two days maximum and that will be it for you... Is that a chance you want to take... please append your signature on the form so that we can proceed... as you can see, we have a busy theater day ahead of us... with ten more surgeries lined up after you..."

"Doctor! It is my life... and it is my legs we are talking about here... not yours! Why don't you give me a chance to choose how and in what form I want to depart this world? Perhaps... you never know... I would prefer to die with my limbs still with me... No matter how rotten they may look now? And yes... doctor... presumably that scale there" pointing to a scale on the corner of the theatre.

"You weigh all that you cut off for proper record keeping and accountability... so after cutting off and weighing my legs... what would you do with them ?"

The theatre had gone silent at this point. The surgeon had lost his patience and his face had gone red. He violently pulled off the surgical gaze he was wearing with a note of stern rebuke on his face.

"So do you want the operation or not?" he asked. Calmly, without emotions, Captain Mondei stared hard at him and responded coolly.

"No... I will not have the operation... I will not have the operation... I will take my chance elsewhere, explore alternatives... and die honourably with all my limbs intact,if I must, yes. I want to return to my creator the way he made me... a complete man... so if you don't mind I want to discharge myself from this hospital right now !"

"Of course... by all means... that is your prerogative. Goodluck in your search for alternatives..." and the surgeon stormed out of the theatre.

Captain Mondei had made arrangements for an exclusive bungalow in the jungle, on the outskirts of San Pedro, near the waterfront. He was wheeled into a waiting military ambulance and driven straight to his new abode. As arranged, Abenaa went over to the bungalow that evening after work.

"You will have to manage with the pains this night... I will give you your anti-biotics and your non-steroidal anti- flamatory drugs for now... and something to make you sleep... Tomorrow and the day after are my off duty days... so we will start the alternative treatment then"

Abenaa arrived at Captain Mondei's new home very early the next morning; and went straight to work. She cut through the massive P.O.P. on the two legs and exposed the flesh. The smell of decay was over-powering. She cleaned and scrubbed the two legs with fresh, newly cut lime and wheeled Captain Mondei outside. She rested the two legs on a stool and squeezed more freshly cut lemon juice on the two legs. "You may go back to sleep. But leave the two legs exposed to the healing powers of pre-dawn dew... It is very wholesome and has healing properties... take a deep breath and let the early morning dew and its therapeutic negative ions soak into the skin of your legs... remain this way whilst I dash into the nearby forest to search for some plants."

Abenaa returned three hours later beaming with smiles.

"We are lucky" She reported with excitement. "I was not too sure... but the African forest is a wonderful reservoir... I found all the plants I would have found back home in Ghana.... Sometime I wonder why God blessed us so much... and to think that we don't even value these gifts!"

She proceeded to unpack her rich harvest... roots ,leaves, stems and barks. When she came to a particular stem, she became very agitated with fulfillment.

"You see this plant... yes this stem" as she cut the skin open... "You see how it bleeds... blood-red liquid.... This is the most important treatment for your legs... we call it "ayam mumuni" in Ghana... When I found it, I knew the Almighty wished you to be healed."

At sunrise, she wheeled Captain Mondei to a makeshift thatched bathroom at the fringe of the vast compound.

"Come,have your therapeutic bath..no matter what your medical situation is... you must have your bath... my father used to say cleanliness is next to Godliness…

"Here…" as she opened a steaming pot of herbs "amankye" leaves for antiseptic cleansing and "akaya" leaves… they will bring your fever down and act as a mild sedative and analgesic for your pains… You will see how you feel after your bath"

It was time for breakfast and Captain Mondei's cook had laid the table with delicacies - fried eggs, bread, milk, marmalade, jam, coffee and butter. Abenaa swept everything off the table.

"From now on… you eat natural foods… that will be part of your natural healing… for breakfast and every meal, you will take a lot of garlic and onions, avocado pears, paw-paw, tomato for lunch, garlic and onions, pineapples complete with the skin, mango, complete with the skin and guava. Dinner will be garlic and onion "efon" leaves soaked in fresh lime juice, coconuts and drink lots and lots of coconut water to detoxify your system."

Except for fresh charcoal – grilled fish eaten freely everday, the strict menu regime was enforced.

In the evening, Abenaa prepared a light charcoal fire on top of which was a metal crossed beam. On top of this beam, she put a perforated flat raffia cane mat. Next on top of the mat she laid plantain leaves, black and red pepper. She soaked Captain Mondei's legs in pure honey and laid them on top of the flat basket of herbs, heated gently from below by the stoking charcoal fire.

After two weeks of treatment, all the signs of infection and inflammation had disappeared and early signs of the growth of a new glowing skin were evident.

At the hospital, the arrival of new expatriate doctors and the transfer of the Medical Director to another project in the Democratic Republic of Congo had occasioned changes. Abenaa was ejected from her tent, which she had occupied at the grace of Doctor Home who actually owned it. As a purely local volunteer, she was expected to source her accommodation and be fully responsible for her own feeding and transportation. She was however to be paid a stipend to cover her expenses. It was in the course of the preparation of these vouchers that her name crept into the local MSF Human Resource Manager's attention in Abidjan. As a local aide to Doctor Home, she had been managed privately from her local stipend. Even her elevation from nursing maid to nursing assistant and now theater assistant were never documented. The HR Manager highlighted these omissions and Abenaa's lack of formal National Registered Nurse(NRN) nursing qualification for her current job.

But the reports from all the doctors she had worked with were exceptionally good. She was rated as an outstanding assistant with initiative, foresight and passionate commitment to humanitarian work. That she had performed creditably and was outstanding beyond her paper qualification raised a dilemma which was quickly resolved by the HR Manager. Abenaa was recommended for a much more formal training before integration into the MSF local staff list. She would be sponsored to an all-expense paid two-year Senior Nursing Course at the Nursing College in Abidjan.

If the new Medical Director had expected joy, gratitude and excitement from "Sister Tessy" when the news of the nursing sponsorship in Abidjan was announced to her, he could not disguise his disappointment. Abenaa politely turned down the offer for "family reasons". She said she had re-integrated with her family members in San Pedro; that the family had come to depend on her for most of their needs and therefore requested to be "passed over" for the opportunity and the resultant promotion. The hospital turned down the request and stressed the consequences of her decision on her tenure; implications that Abenna calmly accepted. There being no need for a formal resignation since she was essentially not on the personnel list of the organization, Abenaa's tenure at the hospital came to an abrupt end as she walked out gracefully through its gate that afternoon.

Captain Mondei had lived for one month, defying the Orthopaedic surgeon's forecast of death in two days unless he had the amputation. He looked and felt healthier and was now lively of spirit. Abenaa now lived within the compound providing medical support to any RUF combatant who happened to come by and asked for help. As she discussed the next line of treatment for Captain Mondei that evening, she brought up a question that had nagged her for a while.

"... I have been wondering... how did you know my name was Abenaa the first time you met me?" Captain Mondei laughed heartily.

"You really want to know the truth?" he asked.

"Yes... yes off course"

"Okay... okay.... It was a wild guess... I guessed it! "

"It's a lie... please you are lying... No... Please tell me the truth!! "

"True... it was an informed guess... Once I established you were Ghanaian from your accent and your faint Ashanti tribal marks... it set me thinking. I am an Intelligence man, remember... a trained observer and a deductive analyst... So I reasoned that... you were Ashanti with an assumed English name – Tessy... so why would you assume that particular name... I searched through in my mind all the popular Ashanti female names for a while and there was none that started with a "T" or sound like Tessy..."

"Hey... you are cheating... how would you know all the Ashanti female names..."

"Common, I am a widely travelled man... I did Basic Infantry and Company Commander's Course at the Ghana Military Academy at Teshie... Of course you can't be at the academy and not socialize with the neighbouring Teshie – Nungua and Tema communities... and I was attached to the Second Battalion in Kumasi for my field training... so you see I know Ghana and the Ashantis quite well..."

"You still have not explained how you came to the conclusion that I was Abenaa" she retorted.

"But you interrupted me... or I was going to come to that" He said jovially.

"Okay, Okay I apologize, please continue"

"Yes... so I deduced that "Tessy" may have jumped naturally to any Ashanti female born on a Tuesday because of the "T" in Tuesday and Tessy... and since the popular Ashanti female names are usually tied to the day of the week the girl is born, I came to the conclusion that Tessy is from Tuesday which is Abenaa for Ashanti female born on Tuesday!"

"Brilliant! Bravo!! ",Abenna exclaimed,holding up her hands. As she did, Mondei involuntarily also held up his hand, and involuntarily, the two hands made contact... and they held hands and embraced for the first time!. As they did, Abenaa felt a jolt of electricity run through her body. Her knees buckled as her heart thumped rapidly. She felt weak, light-headed and dizzy all at once. She recoiled quickly and put up a professional carriage.

"We have work to do... Now that we have cleared the infection and ensured blood flow to your lower limbs once again, we have to commence the delicate task of resetting the bones... I warn you... it is going to be painfully slow and I will require your co-operation at every stage."

"Yes Doctor!!" That was the first time he would fondly refer to her as "doctor", but somehow, the title stuck and the entire camp started referring to the naturally gifted nurse as "doctor" Abenaa.

It was a very painful treatment regimen. Beyond the imagination of Captain Mondei. Besides the sedative given to him to relax his nerves, Abenaa had requested for his three strong personal aides to assist to hold him down during the treatment. Pinned down by the three aides, Abenaa proceeded to use her deft gifted fingers to locate the fractures and the splintered bones. As she felt the bones, the pains ran through the Captain's central nervous system. One by one she located and pushed the displaced bones into position until finally, with a strong pull of the right leg and a sharp aggressive shove, she heard a click as the last splinter fell into place. At this point, the pain had become so excruciating that Captain Mondei slumped into unconsciousness. He was revived with a cold water towel bath and a drink of boiled guava and paw-paw leaves.

When he came to, Abenaa teased him to no end... "I thought you were a strong man? Gosh !... what a low pain threshold you have... a simple bone setting procedure... and you were going to die on us all? Was that why you were so hard on the orthopaedic surgeon at the hospital... because you were afraid of the pain?!"

Captain Mondei was exhausted but he had not lost any of his wittiness and sense of humour.

"I am sure you bewitched me with a magic touch... it must be your own form of local anaesthesia... otherwise how could I.... I, Captain

Abu Mondei, the grandson Menjor, the great, all-conquering Mende warrior collapse like a pack of cards under a woman's caressing fingers..."

"It is a lie!! Tell the truth, you fainted!! Shame... Shame on you
Salieyu"

"You know... talking about that your orthopaedic surgeon at the hospital... I was decidedly hard on him because I wanted to hurt his ego...
I had heard and read so much about his penchant for amputations,
even for the slightest dislocation and sprains... from Grand Bassa to
Conakry... that I was not prepared to make his day by being just another
number on his statistics."

"I see... no wonder you were so harsh... I had never seen you in that
mood before... Good, we will allow you to recover your strength... so
we will leave the left leg till tomorrow evening, but see here" Abenaa said
pointing to, as she took off the palm fronds from the large earthen pot
to reveal the stems of the "ayam-mumuni" now soaked in thick blood
red liquid.

"You see how the liquid looks like blood? I soaked the stems in the
last three weeks in this earthen pot of pure natural honey and ground
periwinkle shells... that's your treatment... You will drink this mixture
and a special broth... I will prepare from dried pepper, dried crayfish,
dried crabs and the twin spices we call "Urhirien" and "erhie"... they are
strong vitalizers and the ground periwinkle shells, crayfish and crabs
will provide the calcium to heal your broken bones..."

Abenaa arranged the stems of the "ayam-mumuni" already cut to size
in a string around the fractured limbs and spread some of the blood-red
liquid over the legs. Gently, but firmly, she bandaged the stems around
the broken leg, with the stems holding the legs and the bones straight
and firm. Next, she wheeled Captain Mondei to the fire-side and lifted
the legs unto the flat raffia mat on top of the simmering fire for the leg
to gently absorb the healing heat and tingling sensation that will return
life to the nerves and muscles. This continued for six more weeks; and
the painful, slow but steady progress towards walking again commenced
with regular physiotherapy exercises. This was nothing short of a miracle; and Abenaa's fame and reputation as an alternative medicine physi-

cian travelled far and wide.

Three months later, Captain Mondei,back on his feet again convinced Abenaa to move with him to the new Revolutionary United Front (RUF) Forward Operating Base near Gbarnga in Liberia. They arrived after a three hour, very uncomfortable Land Rover drive to the field hospital attached to the base.

The next morning, Abenaa, now a living legend was ushered into the large waiting room of Corporal Foday Sankoh. The bumpy terrain she had had to travel to get to Gbarnga had prepared her for a bumpy encounter; given the impressions she had formed from her previous chance encounter with the man all the soldiers call "Papey". When she was finally ushered into the austere office of the Sierra Leonian rebel leader, this scruffy-looking, bearded man stood up from behind a huge mahogany table, walked briskly over to Abenaa and gave her a suffocating bear-hug.

"Welcome to Sierra Leone… in Liberia… this is our temporary home away from home… but I tell you very soon, we will be in Salone… Good…"

As he continued; Abenaa was speechless as she took in the huge man in a rag-tag military fatigue without any form of rank or insignia.

"Doctor… I want to thank you on behalf of all the people of Salone for your wonderful work… we cannot thank you enough for your selfless sacrifice..I want you to continue to work for us… and we will provide you all the material support you need…. Money? Diamond? My gal… I tell you, you won't lack."

Abenaa's protestation that her work was purely humanitarian and that she had no material needs was rebuffed with a brusque wave of the hand. Corporal Sankoh rushed Abenaa to a vacant seat, where he too in an avuncular manner sat uncomfortably next to her. The Corporal, ordinarily not given to expansive personal discussions or romantic outpourings had obviously been overwhelmed by Abenaa's reputation and natural beauty.

"Doctor… you are a good example of what we Africans can do for ourselves… you see where the white man had failed… you have succeeded. The bastards created all these problems for us imposing corrupt minority politicians, cronies and proteges on the original owners of the land. But I tell you with God on our side... We are going to change all that..."

Abenaa was lost.

"Sir, I am not a doctor... I trained..."

"Yes, you are a doctor! What is the duty of a doctor.... Is it not to cure people?... You don't need any paper qualifications from their university to be called a doctor. To us, you are our doctor... what you have done for Captain Mondei confirms that you are a doctor."

Abenaa appraised the Corporal in awe, with subdued, quizzing eyes.

The more she gazed, the more she came to a preliminary conclusion that the Corporal was undoubtedly not the intellectual type; but he was also definitely not an inconsequential or insubstantial character, otherwise he will not have the ability to attract followers like the intelligent Captain Mondei.

What Abenaa did not know at that point was the huge ambition of the man sharing that uncomfortable seat with her. With a fighting force of over five thousand men under his command at that point, he had been able to manipulate international political developments to secure unofficial diplomatic recognition of sorts for his rag-tag army, secured an all-expense paid training facilities for his officers in Libya; established technical working relationships with the leadership of Burkina-Fasso and secured a vital alliance with Area Fada for a staging post for his planned take-over of the leadership of Sierra Leone. All of these he had achieved through native intelligence, avuncular charisma, threats and intimidation and promises of a shared future prosperity built on the immense wealth of Sierra Leone.

What was initially billed to be a courtesy call gradually degenerated into a strident plea for Abenaa to support the fighting forces of the RUF. That she would never regret her decision. It must have been a practical drill, for a man who had repeatedly charmed adolescents into his army with warm avuncular promises of a better tomorrow. Corporal Foday

Sankoh was relaxed and quite informed. He told Abenaa about his student days.

"Just like you... when I was young I wanted things to be done differently... I led revolt after revolt to change the system... and overthrow the entire corrupt politicians in Freetown..."

"That's why they sacked me from the army of Salone. You see, I joined the army to serve my fatherland and to bring about change from the inside.....and the bastards said.... I was planning a coup... me? No way... I only spoke my mind openly at every opportunity..."

He talked about his family, his wife and children.

"I am a family man... I would rather be with my wife and children... but there is work to be done... We must correct the system first... and then the family will have better rights and a better country." As abruptly as it started, the courtesy call was over.. Abenaa was driven back to the field hospital in a convoy of young female combatants. On her return, she found that her quarters had been fully furnished with upholstered chairs, a refrigerator and colour television. Captain Frazier, the Medical Corp Commander took her round the well-stocked field hospital as he formally welcomed her.

As she unpacked more of her personal wares to settle down that afternoon, one of the young female combatants stepped forward, saluted sharply and introduced herself.

"Lance Corporal Habibat Momoh... your ADC reporting for duty Sir!" She had sat with her at the back of the Land Rover during the ride back from the "Papay", but she never really took a second look. But now looking at the dark, young girl smartly dressed in military fatigues, clutching the oversized AK 47 rifle, she shuddered at the sudden turn of events. Habibat could not have been more than fifteen, but the wisened, desperate look in her eyes made her so self assured. As she presented herself on the balcony, with sweat dripping down her brows, the hot tropical sunshine was glinting off her assault rifle. With her still forming breasts straining to burst through the tight uniform, she looked too innocent to be a combatant. Habibat introduced the driver of the Land Rover as Abenaa's driver saluted sharply again and marched off to saunter around the lawn.

She had quickly settled down with Habibat, who was more of a friend now than an ADC. Habibat also doubled as a batman, cleaning, sweeping, washing and running sundry errands. In the evenings, they watched television broadcasts from the Ivory Coast and played scrabble and cards when the signals become too weak on the television, which was usually the case. She was playing a game of cards that evening with Habibat when Captain Mondei stormed in looking excited.

"A very personal present from the Papai..." as he unwrapped a diamond bracelet and presented it to Abenaa.

"But I don't need it... where will I wear it to... here in the bush..."

"It's just a token of appreciation... one day after the war, when all this is over, you will appreciate it..." "Okay, so let's wait for that day..." as she declined the offer'.

"But I can't wait to see you in it... wear it for me... Abenaa, will you marry me?"

The request was unexpected... It jolted Abenaa into a frightening shock of speechlessness. She tried to open her mouth, but was too shocked to be coherent. As Captain Mondei slid into her arms and thrust his lips forward, she managed to say yes quietly. They were married in a very quiet civil ceremony, with only five people present the next day.

They had been married for only two months when "Operation Kuta" rolled off on two fronts into Sierra Leone. An RUF column rolled across the Manu River and struck Pendenbru whilst a pincer movement overran Kailahun and headed straight towards the very vital Tongo diamond fields, with a medium-term objective of capturing Koidu.

Captain Mondei had been particularly pleased with himself for being the prime mover of the offensive. Earlier during the week, he had presented an Intelligence evaluation of the Liberia offensive to "GK" the RUF's fond name for Area Fada. Mondei had emphasized that to expect a final capture of Monrovia and an effective take over of the government of Liberia before embarking on the Sierra Leonian operation was a poor strategy. He contended that ECOMOG was growing in strength and fire-power and with the ECOMOG mission mandate having been changed from "peace keeping" to "peace enforcement" ECOMOG was pushing harder especially with increased air support; the ECOMOG Air Task Force was based at the Lungi International Airport in Freetown. Therefore, Captain Mondei's proposed codename for the mission - Operation Kuta,- "Kuta being the strong" Sierra Leonian smoked fish whose little portion filled the mouth to over-flowing proportions was aptly descriptive of the primary objective of the mission: To broaden the theater of operation by opening two new fronts in Sierra Leone, thereby stretching the resources of ECOMOG; weaken ECOMOG's defence of Liberia, especially of the capital Monrovia; and make the town vulnerable to NPFL capture thereby; and finally provide additional sources of war funding from Sierra Leone with the capture of the Tongo diamond fields.

The plan was approved and with additional troop reinforcements by a composite battalion offered by "GK", "Operation Kuta" was very successful.

The main attack accomplished all its strategic objectives in the first one week of battle. Mopping up operations continued for another one week, with the establishment of Forward Operating Bases in the outskirts of Daru and Yengema. The first RUF Supreme Command Headquarters was established at "Camp Eleven"

Six months after Operation Kuta, the RUF having mastered the terrain and more battle-tested, commenced a big south-westerly move.

As the reports filtered back to Mission Control headquarters, the atmosphere in Camp Eleven that night was boisterous. What was planned as an initial reconnaissance mission to the diamond rich Kono district had proven to be a rich harvest. The Strike Force had penetrated the entire Sierra Leonian army defences and moved into central Sefadu. Caught unawares, the very popular Opera cinema, which was showing the third run of Bruce Lee's. Enter the Dragon that night was rocked by a purely speculative explosion. Then panic took over. From the Opera Cinema, rumour of a massive invasion force led by armored columns headed towards the city centre from Makeni spread rapidly. The Sierra Leone army garrison, located at the northerly – tip of the town upon hearing of the take over of the city centre felt cut-off, isolated and voted with their feet. A detachment of the special police crack force, the SD unit rallied round to locate and fight the enemy, but ran head-on into the RUF strike force ambush by the junction of 555 spot. The fighting was very brief as the darkness amplified the armament and personnel strength of what was really a small Recce squad. With the two SD Land Rovers and their occupants pulverized, the entire town was thrown into wild speculations on the scale and direction of the next RUF attack. Rumours of a huge deluge took over, with resultant sapped morales. Commandeering of civilian vehicles became rampant as military person-nel scrambled on any available vehicle to flee; encouraged by rapid burst of gun fire, mostly fired into the air by the RUF.

In response, the Sierra Leone Army lavished rounds of gun fire at the unseen enemy thereby exacerbating the panic. Over the night, there was rampant looting, house-to-house burning and amputation of stragglers. At the command of the adjunct NPFL commander, more hackings and amputations were undertaken. The development marked the beginning of the "Long-Sleeve and Short Sleeve" amputation offensive - a stubborn and uncooperative civilian had his hands cut above the elbow whilst more pliable ones had their hands cut above their wrists.

By the next morning, a fresh RUF battalion had jumped off its Forward Operating Base to mop up and garrison the town. The joy and dancing around Camp Eleven was infectious. In a macabre war dance, the combatants danced with the decapitated head of the SD unit com-mander in Kono.

"Who say we no go conquer" was bellowed... and followed by a huge chorus"

"Na lie... we don conquer!"

That evening, there was a marked hushed atmosphere around the camp as a meeting of the Supreme RUF Council held. Abu Kanu and Rashid Mansarray, two experienced combatants who trained with the Papei in Libya and whose youthful charisma and contacts mobilized students union and youth movements for the support of the RUF were at Camp Eleven for the meeting.

The meeting was dominated by Intelligence Reports presented by Captain Mondei: Pa Djalloh, a long serving steward at the British High Commission chancery and a Long-established mole of the RUF and another ECOMOG source had confirmed imminent attacks on Camp Eleven. Satellite and aircraft reconnaissance photos obtained from other agents confirming the ECOMOG Fighter Command's interest in Camp Eleven were discussed. The Supreme Council agreed at the meeting that the three high profile prisoners should be moved rapidly from camp to camp to confuse and negate any plan for a surgical military strike to release them.

The second Intelligence report was more contentious. Captain Mondei reported that the RUF stood for justice and the good life for the people of Sierra Leone. Years of deprivation, hunger and disease virtually unnoticed by the outside world because of the antics and flamboyance of corrupt politicians had so far been exposed by the propaganda efforts of the RUF. But how can the RUF claim to be a corrective regime when they themselves now prey on innocent civilians, commit appalling bestial violence against the same people that they claim to represent… just under one year into operations in Sierra Leone, the report queried. Captain Mondei then showed photo reels of amputations, house burnings, rapes, lootings… not just by the other ranks, but also by officers!.

The heavily fortified cave where the meeting was held was thrown into silence. Everyone around the meeting room knew about these developments, but some had been too scared to speak out. But those opposed to the scare tactics were in the minority in Mondei, Kanu and Mansaray. One after the other, they spoke out strongly against the poor value system and orientation of the troops and the need for unit commanders to take responsibility for the discipline of their troops. With the possibility of the meeting degenerating into name calling, the avuncular and charismatic Corporal Foday Sankoh, held up his hands and cut in brusquely:

"I am in charge of this army… whatever atrocities, committed by my army… I take full responsibility… that is the mark of a leader… not finger- pointing and pontification… I have listened to the Intelligence report and heard all the arguments… I will investigate and take appropriate actions in due course… meeting dismissed!"

Camp Forty-Four was a fort and a haven of sorts. Tucked into the bowels of the Sula Mountains, a network of underground tunnels connected the very dense Tonkolili forest. On the north-westerly side of the camp was the Bumbuna stream, which led upstream to the Bumbuna water falls. It was to this naturally fortified camp that the RUF Supreme Command Headquarters. was transferred after the Supreme Military Council Meeting. After the long tabbing to the new camp, the high profile prisoners were referred to the field hospital for full medical checks. Squadron Leader Ikeke, Captain Denning and Sergeant Burden were allotted an inner recess in the cave next to the medical section for specialized care.

Abenaa had been briefed already about the clavicular fracture of the Nigerian pilot and the fractured thigh bone of the British paratrooper. She read through their cases and promptly commenced the treatment plan as instructed by Dr.Frazier.

Mammy Kankay was the leader of the "Semas" and the soon to be initiated in the Bush School. The Tinkoko Bondo Society had chosen her to lead their annual Bush School on account of her vast experience. First, she had seven children of her own; she was an experienced Traditional Birth Attendant (TBA) and she was the leader of the female folk drama group. That night, as she led the girls in songs, she recalled her own initiation rites. Then, she recalled, you had to be mature, with a full breast to prove it before you could make the camp. But the girls get too street wise, too quickly these days that if you wait for their full maturity, before enlistment into the Bondo society, it might be too late... they could get pregnant and too worldly for the strict discipline of the Bush School. There was also the strictly financial consideration, she thought. When the girls are still young, the pressure is less on the mother to buy clothes, jewelry, shoes and other initiation items because the small girls are not very worldly and are appreciative of the little gestures from their parents.

Presently, Mammy Kankay raised the chorus of another Temni song and the three other supporting elderly ladies echoed a spontaneous response in unison. As the elders sang and clapped, the young initiates were gradually inducted into the singing. After a while, the children were encouraged to lead the songs themselves under observation. The Bush School taught everything a growing girl needed to know: Changes in her body as she grew, pregnancy and birth, nursing a baby, singing, dancing, cooking, basic hygiene and menstrual care, traditional medicines and herbs, oral tradition and history, everything.

That night, they were not only taught the songs, but the dance steps and the backing percussions. They also learnt the Bondo code of honour, secrecy, proverbs and coded communication. The oil lanterns dotting the thick forest and the huge cave where the Bush School held created the additional mystique required by the Bondo society to enforce conformity. This mysterious spot deep into the forest which the people of Tinkoko call "Yanka" or cave had served as the Bondo sacred grove for over two hundred years. There were over thirty girls in the "Yanka" that night. As they sang and clapped in unison, Mammy Kankay led the other women to share the "patronage" leaf round the girls: They were to chew the leaves which acted to sedate and reduce their anxiety before the crucial circumcision rites the next day: At about midnight, the "digbas -" elderly native surgeons- who would perform the circumcisions the next morning arrived.

The excitement and anxiety that greeted the arrival of the "digbas" had hardly died down, than a loud male voice echoed through the "Yanka" for everyone to stand up. As the order was given, more heavy thuds of military boots echoed round the cave as they flooded into the "Yanka"

"Unu Kushe-o!"

The RUF sergeant who led the squad bellowed. The accoustic force of his unaccustomed male voice in this strictly female setting; and the loud echo from the bowels of the "Yanka" brought shock and awe to the young girls, who now desperately cluttered around their "Semas" and "digbas" for protection. The sergeant assured them, they would not hurt anybody; if they all co-operated that is. But the darting eyes of the NPFL second-in-command was not re-assuring at all, as he took in the bare cleavages of the girls. Mammy Kankay saw the lust and drug induced exuberance of the second-in-command and stepped in quickly to take charge.

"Abomination! Abomination!" she screamed.

"This is a sacred Bondo grove... handed down to us by our grand – mothers... as it was handed down to them by their great – grand mothers... abomination!... No male has ever stepped unto this sacred soil... no male... soldier or no soldier... we have no problem with any- body... so you will move out of this "Yankah" with your backs... Now step backwards and back-out all the way out of the "Yankah" that is the only remedy for this abomination... Now!"

As some of the soldiers made to obey and retreat as ordered, the sec-ond-in-command barked out in his native Liberian slang.

"No way... I say me men... are you crazy... ?" as he corked his AK47. Now emboldened, the rest of the unit stood firm as they all took firing postures.

With loud shouts, curses and protestations from the "digbas" and "semas", the soldiers took time to line up the shivering initiates and marched them out in single file. Before their departure, the second-in-command retuned to the cave to give the old women the "short-sleeve" treatment.

The news hit Tinkoko the next day. The abduction of thirty young Bondo society initiates by the RUF; and the cruel amputation of the supervising "digbas" and "semas" who tried in vain to stop them. By the time, help was rushed from the village to the "Yankah", it was too late for Mammy Kankay. She had bled to death. The RUF strike on the neighboring village of Matturu was even deadlier. All the young men and women were led out into the bush and straight into RUF camps, whilst the elderly were given an assortment of "short-sleeve" and "long-sleeve" treatments; and bonfires made of their homes.

Captain Mondei had a reputation for strict professionalism. His hand-picked "Delta Romeo Foxtrot" was built as a Deep Recce Force that could operate independently in small fifty- man squads; with capability to fight its way out of any situation. With a total strength of just under two hundred men, operating in squads of fifty, The Deep Recce Force was trained and nurtured personally by the captain. A network of moles and informants that spread all the way to the Presidency, the embassies and ECOMOG complemented this crack squad that could match any in the world in jungle insurgency and field intelligence gathering.

Mondei's ideological zeal which manifested long ago at the Mount Aureal home of the Fourah Bay College's Sierra Leone Socialist Students Movement (SSM) was further honed during his military training stint in Libya. His Deep Recce Force reflected his ideological leanings: A frugal life style, abhorrence of wealth and material possessions, strong, disciplined communal values. He ran an almost egalitarian army, where he would spend time with the rank and file discussing their personal needs and battle plans. He taught his men the best survival tricks of the jungle. He used to jokingly say that Africans spoil for wars because they are so richly blessed. That's why historical ethnic wars raged on and on and you wondered why there were so many survivors afterwards. Because the jungles and forests of Africa are so richly endowed, communities on the run from their enemies could actually live off the ground in the forests, procreate and prosper for years. The modern jungle warrior had to learn from and improve on that, he always told his men. Mondei taught his men the importance of keeping themselves clean and healthy always. Every soldier in his force must boil his water before drinking. Faeces must be passed into a small hole and neatly covered with earth.

He taught them the capability of the human body when well cared for with good food, vitamins and regular exercises. An army that fought on an empty stomach was a doomed army, he would teach. He always managed to get multi-vitamin tablets supply for his men who are enjoined to take daily doses. He marched with his men always, ensuring adequate supply of the country's staple food and the principal source of nourishment- rice. The force carried well-smoked meat in pouches. So dry and so well-smoked that a very small piece when chewed or boiled with rice will be extremely filling indeed. Whatever the jungle could provide by way of nourishment they made use of; and there were abundant sources in wild-growing berries, bananas, plantains, cherries and so many more wild fruits. Malaria was endemic in the country, so every soldier in his unit was enjoined to drink the local malaria broth produced from boiling some local herbs regularly as a prophylactic.

He taught his men to wash and dry their uniforms at every opportunity, keep their marching boots clean and dry, especially their socks. All weapons must be cleaned and oiled at every rest point during tabbing. Mondei taught his men survival tricks in the jungle. Animal hunting and trapping tricks adapted for guerilla warfare, marching in circuits to avoid leaving trails, bamboo booby traps and many more tricks.

Captain Mondei was at a Night Stop with his HQ squad of fifty men around the vicinity of Daru when he received the distress call on his open line. Apparently, the well-planned assault on Pujehun had all gone wrong. Reinforcements from the Nigerian battalion in Bo had been rushed in overnight to bolster the Sierra Leone army garrison and the entire 7th Battalion of the RUF was now encircled. By the time he managed to get the details from the RUF battalion commander, over half of the battalion had been wiped out and the other half pinned down with sustained gunfire. Although the details were sketchy, it was obvious that what was planned as a two-pronged attack on Pujehun, with the 202 battalion providing the rear pincer attack from the north-west had not materialized.

Reports were to indicate later that the attack was launched by the 7th battalion from the South-East as planned at 23.00 hours. After initial gains by the 7th and effective occupation of the outlying surburbs of the town, the expected rear and flank attacks from the 202 battalion failed to materialize. The Sierra Leone army garrison with reinforcements from Bo launched an encirclement counter-attack. The RUF 7th battalion commander swore and cursed all night in Creole on the open radio at how he had been let-down and sabotaged by the 202 when Captain Mondei cut off the transmission.

Captain Mondei tabbed at a fast pace with his men all night arriving the outskirts of Pujehun to the North-West early that morning. He appraised the situation, conscious of the heavy firing and use of high caliber mortars and artillery in the raging battle. Knowing that a direct assault on the enemy could be futile with his comparatively weak strength and armament, he opted for a desperate commando attack on the main garrison to spread panic in the town and free the RUF 7th battalion.

He stormed the town's police station and commandeered two available trucks; and forced the duty officer to broadcast an SOS, that a strong RUF force of over three battalion strength had been sighted advancing from Bo. The message was repeated over and over.

In a lightning speed, the squad crashed through the perimeter defences and drove to the garrison headquarters, firing sporadically. Next, the armoury located to the end of the barracks under a mango tree and covered in tarpaulin was struck. The explosion tore and shook the entire town. By now, the entire garrison and the garrison's command and control had been overtaken by fear and panic. Urgent criss-crossing radio communications ripped through the air in panic. Suddenly with the explosions, the main radio mast of the garrison headquarters was ripped apart, severing all communication links with the forces in the front lines, the Forward Operating Bases and army HQ. in Freetown. That development marked the end of any organized Sierra Leone Army resistance and the end of a coherent defence of Pujehun. In droves, soldiers threw away their weapons and uniforms and slipped away.

Captain Mondei re-established contact with the grateful commander of the 7th battalion. With his strength substantially reduced to less than a hundred men, they both reasoned, it would be tactically unwise to press the attack along the initial lines of effective occupation. The mission was converted to a commando raid and all strategic installations of any military significance were destroyed before their hasty but organized retreat into the jungle.

The Supreme Ruling Council of the RUF usually met once every fort-night. But this was an emergency meeting called to review recent military operations. The huge cave which served as the Council's Meeting Room was already packed full when the Supreme Commander, Corporal Foday Sankoh sauntered in amid shouts of "Papei, Papay... Papa Morlai..." A wave of excitement rented the air as he made his way to the head of the table. Without ceremonies and without reading from prepared notes, he gave an update on developments.

"The war is progressing as planned on all fronts. You already have a Sitrep on the the capture of Kamajor leaders in Yengedugu and Kpanba. All ten of them have been executed! We pressed on with our attacks; with the capture of Seghwema and probing attacks on Kenema to assess the enemy strength in the town. Gerinhun was also captured and held for one week to prevent strategic supplies and reinforcement from Bo to Kenema. In the Northern Sector, we have captured Koinadugu and we are right now massing troops for a major assault on Kabala." Corporal Sankoh paused for effect.

He continued.

".... Our offensive on the diplomatic front is going very well. The ECOWAS leaders now recognize and talk to us;and a Peace and Reconcilliation Conference under the auspices of ECOWAS is planned for Abuja,Nigeria later this month. We maintain supremacy on the BBC Africa Service. We intend to press on with this momentum, with broadcast of interviews with the captured enemy officers and mercenar-ies in due course. We are expecting fresh supplies of arms and ammu-nition; including some SAM-7 missiles to keep these "dudu birds" off, our backs. The struggle continues! And victory is assured!! There was a rapturous round of applause around the hall, even before he had uttered the last chant.

Then silence descended on the room.

"Papei Sir"

Captain Mondei called out from the end of the room as he cleared his voice to speak; and standing to attention to salute the Supreme Commander.

"Here… sir, you already have my intelligence reports from all the sectors. The war is not going right at all."

"Is that so… why do you say that?" Corporal Sankoh retorted.

"Sir, it depends on what our benchmark for success is… When we started… we had a mission to bring the good life to our people… we said we will root out corruption… give freedom and equality to all the citizens of Sierra Leone… remember sir, we argued that despite our huge diamond resources, we had been plundered to become one of the poorest countries in the world… that corruption, unequal distribution of wealth, nepotism, tribalism and the Freetown/Provincial divide in the affairs of the country had created huge gaps that the RUF must address…"

There was now absolute silence. Captain Mondei continued.

"We are now fighting a war that is not grounded on any idealogical value or a discernible central mission statement.Our soldiers now operate without core disciplinary values.The RUF is gradually being perceived as an army of occupation. Our soldiers have gradually imbibed the NPFL's negative systematic scorched earth policy and have become so indisciplined that officer command and control roles are being hijacked by other ranks. How can we be seen as messiahs by our people when we are busy mutilating and decapitating them? Here…" as he passed round, photographs

"Sir, the photographs you are looking at… were innocent citizens of the Republic of Sierra Leone, law-abiding… weighed down for years by the oppressive regimes in Freetown… and suddenly the RUF comes… not as messiahs but as butchers… Look at this elderly man of over seventy….. our tradition teaches us to respect age… how this old man could possibly have hurt anyone is doubtful… his two arms were chopped off in Tomboudou!! At Nemessedu, the entire male population was wiped out and all the young girls raped and abducted… In Koidu, this young man, an undergraduate with a promising life ahead of him had his two arms chopped off. Reason: He was too tall and too handsome… will attract all the pretty girls!!!"Captain Mondei paused for a glass of water and continued.

"In Sinekoro town near Kabalah, an entire congregation at a church was roasted alive. Sir... our children... our future... the main reason for our revolution is to give them a better future are being systematically targeted... Our children are being murdered, tortured, raped and enslaved for sexual purposes... here... a report from Tinkoko of the invasion of the most sacred Bondo society's "Yankah"... Every Sierra Leonian is brought up to respect the "Yankah" as a sacred ground that is strictly forbidden for men to step on... we respect the initiation rites of our young girls... and to trample on our traditions in the name of the RUF!!"

"Enough! Stop it... !! Captain, we are fighting a war you know... weren't you taught in your Terrorism Basics that you have to spread the fires and sufferings of hell to create the peace and tranquility of heaven... ?"

"But we are not a terrorist organization, sir! We are Liberators, Nationalists, we made that distinction from the beginning... I don't know what others say they are... but I am definitely not a terrorist!!

"That is semantics... It is all this Fourah Bay grammatical noise... we are fighting a war period.!! And all means are fair as long as you give me results!... Yes... Major Sesay... you have your hands up... you wanted to say something... ?"

Major Abu Kanu-Sesay, the Nigerian Defence Academy trained Commanding Officer of the 7th battalion and of the recent near-fiasco Puyehun attack, stood to ramrod attention and saluted smartly.

"Sir! Like many others here, I am concerned about the growing negative influence of the Liberian NPFL soldiers in our midst... In many cases, we have seen strong indications that we don't share the same military and political objectives..."

"Major!" The Papay quickly cut in "why don't you speak for yourself... and stick to the facts!"

"Yes Sir! Let me speak for myself and my village then..." A Muffled chuckle went round the room. "One year ago when we commenced hostilities, I was received as a hero, a liberator when I returned to my village. Not anymore. Today, the RUF, especially the NPFL component of it has destroyed all that" From his briefcase, he brought out a photo album compiled secretly by the village photographer of the stage-by-stage brutalization of the women of Gandorhun.

"Here" the major continued "Gang rape of an entire family... brothers forced to rape sisters... sons forced to rape mothers... the men and the old women shot thereafter and the young girls taken away as porters and sex slaves... !" silence.

"Sir" he continued... here" thrusting a photograph at the room, the family photograph of a happy, smiling family.Now,that family is gone... see how the entire family is stripped naked in the next photograph... see the NPFL insignias of the soldiers... see the raw animalistic behaviour as one of them pounces on and mounts that girl(pointing at a photograph now) that couldn't be more than ten years old... Sir! See how after raping and exhausting their energies on our innocent girls, this one actually pokes a stick into the vagina of this innocent girl... can you just visualize and imagine the pains this girl would have gone through? It is the same story everywhere... abduction, rape, forced labour, sexual slavery, mutilation, amputation, house burnings, lootings... I could go on and on and all of these crimes committed in the name of the RUF... in our name!"

"Point of correction major! Not in our name... but in 'my' name... don't forget I still run this army and I am man enough to take responsibility for the acts of every man in this army... Okay?"

"Yes sir! That brings me to my main issue... Operation Tarawally"

At the mention of this disastrous operation in Pujehun, there were hushed murmurs across the room... and absolute silence descended

"Somebody has to take responsibility for my loss of over eight hundred men in one day! Somebody will need to explain why the Liberian 2i/c of the 202 battalion stopped the battalion from joining the attack as planned; and thereby exposed the entire 7th battalion to total annihilation..."

"Stop!... I say stop this finger pointing!... it will not bring back your fallen men... it will not! So why dwell on the past... you should charge yourself to build even a better fighting force in their memory... The 202 battalion... Yes. I take responsibility for their actions... I understand

they were required urgently elsewhere for a more strategic operation...
so I gave my approval!"

At that point, an absolute mortuary silence descended upon the
room. This was the first official confirmation of what seemed to be
mere rumours before now of the Papay's role in the Pujehun fiasco. It
confirmed the stories going round the units that Papay was more inter-
ested in the diamond fields than any eventual political and military victory that will give the RUF total control of the country. It confirmed the
secret alliance between the Papay and the NPFL elements in RUF to
concentrate the forces around the mine fields. It confirmed the regular
NPFL – led convoys to Liberia to deliver diamonds from the RUF.

"Sir!" It was the deep- throated imperial voice of Major 'Manny
Rashid'

"Can you confirm that the 202 battalion was diverted to the Tongo
Diamond Fields to protect a Liberian-Lebanese miner... and that the
same battalion is even now charged with convoy protection for the same
Lebanese diamond miner?"

"No Major!!"

"Can you then confirm the total value of the diamonds the RUF has
exported to Liberia since we re-entered Sierra Leone?"

"No"

"How much is it costing us to prosecute this war... and how much
contribution are we getting from friendly nations!"

The Papei could not take it anymore. His authority and leadership
were being questioned openly and he was not going to have any of that.
Not anymore

"Major... I think you have made your point... please sit down!"

"Sir!... I have not quite finished making my point..." "I say sit down...
will you? What's happening here? Let's not forget we are running a
disciplined army here... who exactly is in charge of this army? Let me
remind you... just in case you have forgotten... That piece of uniform
on you... that service revolver in that brand new holster... those shinny
boots and the food you eat everyday... I provide them all. Sit down! Let
me educate you! You cannot fight a war without food... without guns...

without ammunition…. without men… without diplomacy… without propaganda and the deft manipulation of the media… I provide all that… because I am in charge… Yes I have the big picture… and I focus on that big picture to deliver the final result. Not you. Not anyone here. And whilst at it… who gave us the jump-off position for our attack? Who gives us international access to a sea port for our exports and our vital military supplies? Whose communication facilities sustain our propaganda machine… who is right now training our next generation of fighters?… You know the answers. At least, I credit you with enough intelligence to provide the answers yourselves. We will win this war. But not with constant distractions like these… But with everyone playing his assigned role… not meddling… and through honest and transparent loyalty and commitment to the RUF cause and of course the RUF leadership. Thank you all. Dismissed"

That evening at the Main Quadrangle of the camp, it was the usual ebullient, charismatic and chummy Foday Sankoh that was on display. That evening, like many other evenings before, he had brought himself down to the level of the foot soldiers and the impoverished youths in the camp as a rallying social point. He sat on a raffia mat that evening like everyone else and was the chief story teller in the "domei", a traditional oral narrative that the Mendes had made very popular. With simple plots and themes of moral values, good and evil, the contents had been adapted and enriched to include themes of heroism, valour and honour to suit the moral build-up of the RUF. In story after story, the role of the "ndeba" (the protective spirits of the dead) and the "kekeni" the family ancestral spirits were woven into traditional narratives. Together, the two traditional spirits constituted the "ndeebla" who are woven into tales of gallantry by the folk channel propaganda tales of the RUF to demonstrate ancestral and spiritual support for the rebellion and its human cost. That evening, Foday Sankoh was the charismatic "kpakoisia", the oldest, most respected and fluent linguist who gave a narrative account of the origin of the Mende nation by a hunter/warrior. The crafty Papa Morlai at his devious best had that night assumed the role of the "Poro" elder statesman with a key educational function to bring up young Mende men into traditional and military arts and to conduct them through the rites of passage into adulthood. The normal structure and sequence of a Poro society initiation was now closely intertwined with the evening's "domei" entertainment.

The non-initiates around the quadrangle which included Abenaa, and the three special prisoners of war watched and enjoyed the entertainment value without recognizing the spiritual indoctrination that Foday, the grandmaster had initiated. Deep rituals and symbolic languages which should normally only be deployed in the "Kpanguima" – the official secret lodge of the "Sande" - the official initiation forest -were intermingled with rituals of valour to create a cult following for the Papay. The crafty leader was aware of the enormous influence of the "Poro" and "Sande" secret societies in Mende culture; how they provided elements of strict control and weighty sanctions for transgressions. They lay down rules of conduct and provided the thorough formal and informal influence and the relevant pressure to control secular institutions and disciplinary conduct. Once initiated into the Poro secret society, the young men will remain members for life and will be responsible for promulgation and enforcement of traditional decrees.

The sacred bond of the "Poro",its emphasis on a sworn oath of secrecy and silence were considered golden. All new initiates took an oath of silence. All of these cultural institutions and values had been manipulated to serve the Papay very well; and he had integrated his military hierarchy and control into the Poro traditions for absolute loyalty. Thus, as he spoke in the Poro secret language and made secret signs with all the initiates, the stage was set for the "domei" for the night whose moral was on the rewards of treachery.

"Kpa... Kpa... itaye!"

"Yeah!" The crowd responded.

"Kpa... Kpa... Itaye!"

"Yeah" the crowd responded again in unison.

It was Vandie, one of Papay's most trusted personal body guards, and a very nimble and fleet - footed "domei" performer that was at the centre of the quadrangle that night. Vandei developed his "domei" out of the popular folkloric ever-present tortoise as he painted the image of greed, ambition, treachery and eventual retribution. The deceptive tortoise was presented in human form as a man who over-reached himself because he was too clever by half. The "domei" by Vandie presented a very caring father-in-law who invited Mr. Tortoise to a great feast in heaven. But the ungrateful tortoise upon sighting the variety and richness of the feast in heaven decided to take all the food in heaven for himself... He presented himself deceptively as "Mr. All-of-You" And so, it was that as the feast was served in heaven, all the delicious meals were served ostensibly for "all of you" which in that case was Mr. Tortoise. It was not too long before the in-laws discovered Mr. Tortoise's treachery. He was promptly thrown all the way from heaven. Wingless, he crashed to earth and his shell was broken up all over;and that's why the tortoise still carried those cracked scars even till date! Vandei's narrative was inter-spaced with assumed dialogues and songs in the great "domei" tradition. As the deceptive tortoise overfed himself, Vandei assumed the pose of a glutton gradually bloating up and becoming pregnant. The trickery and gluttony displayed by Mr.Tortoise was dramatised through a plaintive duet between tortoise and the heavenly masters... "Masters... masters... masters... the food you just put on the table... here... please who is it meant for... ?" "O, my earthly visitors please eat to your fill the food is for "all of you!" Turning to his in-laws, he would re-echo the directive of the heavenly masters. "They say it is for "all of you... which means it is for me... I am sure yours must be on the way"

The inevitable revelation of Mr. Tortoise's trickery and the final recognition of his treachery by the heavenly masters and his in-laws; was followed by their united desire to mete out justice and punishment on a now hapless tortoise. As they beat up tortoise, his song is re-adapted....

"Master... masters,... masters... When you give your daughter to a greedy man... who steals and cheats you repeatedly.... Won't you beat him, make him wingless and crash him against the hard earth?" "Oh, my earthly visitors, please beat him... strip him... banish him... a treacherous in-law... ? Even God himself forbids it!"

Even in the midst of the highly entertaining "Domei" performance, Papa Morlai was planning, scheming and ordering the final solutions to get rid of his perceived disloyal officers. The choice of the "domei" imagery as an avenue for folk communication and signaling had always been recognized in Mende society. But its use by Foday Sankoh, who through the various theatrical performances functioned as a didactic medium reflecting the multiple influence of the RUF state was not lost on the initiated. Above all, the internal dynamics and personal visions of the Papay made the "domei" more than just another night of entertainment: The sub-plots within the domei underscored the valence of the imageries and the ability of the underlying themes to impact the main domei storylines and the adaptability of these story lines to substitutions and malleability became the central intrigue that drove the hidden meanings of what essentially was an open plot. The real performer that night at the 'domei" was the Papay himself; who had the paternal and avuncular stature to influence the storylines and their symbolism. The moral for the night therefore was that treachery and disloyalty had consequences.

It took all of four months to plan.

Enough time for the suspicions and amimosities to evaporate. But the end was inevitable. The opportunity for Staff College training at the Benghazi Defence Academy was too good to overlook. With a special emphasis on Composite Battalion Command and Control and Counter-Terrorism tactics, the six-month long course, came with lucrative allowances in foreign exchange and opportunity for field management of an RUF fighting division post-graduation; complete with composite units of armour, infantry, logistic, ordinance, intelligence, artillery, planning and staff duties.

Expectedly, the competition for the six available slots was fierce; forc-

ing the RUF High Command to organize screening/written pre-quali-
fication tests and individual presentations on military tactics. After a
grueling week-long screening, six successful officers including Mondei,
Rashid and Kanu-Sesay were unanimously selected for the Course in
Benghazi.The six officers were accorded very elaborate departure ceremonies at Camp Eleven, Twenty-Two and Forty-Four;and highlighted
by the "Papay" as the bright new hope;and the next generation of Sierra
Leone leadership upon their return from Libya.

The journey through Kailahun into Lofa county, en-route Gharnga
and thence to Abidjan to catch the Balkan Airlines flight to Tripoli
was smooth. They were well into Lofa county in Liberia by the out-
skirt of Gandorhun when the convoy of six jeeps ran into the ambush.
Details were not immediately clear. But reports later suggested that a
night before, elements of Roosevelt Johnson's ULIMO forces had moved
from Bo in Sierra Leone and seized the town of Gandorhun... But at
the Local Divisional Office, the heavily fortified residence of the local
NPFL commander, a battle raged between ULIMO and NPFL forces
overnight. The NPFL position was reinforced overnight by Area Fada's
Special Commando Force, a headquarters reserve company based in
Gbarnga under the direct command of the notorious drug addict and
Area Fada's very staunch loyalist, Captain "Monkey Business". The
Captain whose ostensible mission was the recapture of Gandorhun and
the assassination of Roosevelt Johnson, who reportedly led the attack
had other plans.

With his company-strong force of battle-hardened commandos, he
struck through the town's main road and quickly established an effective
cordon; whilst eliminating the initial ULIMO resistance.

But as he pushed forward, "Monkey Business" and his men reportedly
encountered very heavy opposition from Roosevelt Johnson's personal
guards and began to take heavy casualties as the commandos fought
their way through. When it appeared that the counter-attack was in
jeopardy and was being repulsed rapidly, he ordered a tactical retreat to
the entrance to the town and set up a three level ambush, fortified and
heavily camouflaged;... with clear instructions to all his section leaders

to shoot at sight anyone who came through the ambush.

According to later reports, all of which lacked detail and context, it was precisely the next morning; with the ULIMO already in retreat and far-away from the combat area, that the RUF convoy of six jeeps drove straight into the ambush. It was a hopeless situation. The RUF convoy shouted their identity and password in vain. Caught in the three level cross ambush;and with their identification calls ignored, the RUF convoy returned fire fiercely and tried to fight their way through the ambush. Ferocious and prolonged fighting lasted till dawn. The RUF convoy,outnumbered and caught in a poor tactical shooting position was eventually over-powered after further hard fighting, during which its six officers who were en-route the Benghazi Course were killed.

As the NPFL continued final mopping up operations, careful not to leave any witnesses of what they knew was an assasination, Captain Mondei's body guards opened a last burst of fire which hit Captain "Monkey Business" at several spots. He died instantly. The death of "Monkey Business", the unintended outcome of a master-stroke that was designed to eliminate the three disloyal RUF officers gave credence to the version of the story that was spread immediately after the ambush: That Roosevelt Johnson's personal elite unit had attacked a convoy of RUF and NPFL officers, inflicting very heavy casualties, including Captains "Monkey Business" Mondei, Kanu-Sesay and Rashid.

With the three prisoners of war blind-folded, the convoy rode through the jungle. A jungle of thick rain and mangrove forest. They traversed the jungle through a narrow bumpy foot-path barely wide enough for the jeeps to squeeze through. On either side, dense under bush, treacherous green expanse of forest that had swallowed many combatants in previous battles. They made a bend and behind it a dozen large logs blocked the path. The convoy stopped for identification as heavily armed and camouflaged RUF soldiers screened the occupants as they requested for the day's password. They moved on and descended a steep incline as the valley widened and as they trudged through charred remains of vehicles and putrid human remains. Such was the grotesque outlook and rampant deaths that the putrid stench of human decay persisted.

They forged through a shallow stream; and finally, after six grueling hours, the convoy arrived at the secret location, where the "Papei" and a white man were waiting. The blind folds were removed and the prisoners were formally introduced. Under the thick under-bush; in the bowels of a hilly out-crop, the white man introduced himself....

"Robert Black... BBC Africa Service" he announced, stretching his hands forward for handshakes. He too had had to travel for over forty-eight hours. When he was told the interview had been approved by the RUF High Command by its Liaison Officer way back in Abidjan, little did he realize that he would have to travel blind-folded through some of the most bumpy forest paths in the world to get the prized interview. Forty-eight hours after, armed with his portable Uher tape recorder, he was face-to-face with the two British soldiers and the Nigerian fighter – pilot; the first person outside of the RUF to set eyes on them since their capture.

With pleasantries exchanged, Robert Black went straight to business.

"Foday Sankoh, the story is that these prisoner were abducted by your men... when do you intend to release them ?"

"Abducted? They were all enemy combatants captured in battle... and now taken as Prisoners of War" the Papay retorted.

".Captain Denning... what were you possibly doing in Sierra Leone... so far from your home base... and how did you get yourself into combat and eventual capture by the RUF?", the BBC reporter asked.

"I am part of a military training mission in Sierra Leone by virtue of an Anglo – Sierra Leone Millitary Pact... I am a trainer... not a combatant... I was abducted in Freetown, very far away from the theatre of conflict... I cannot possibly be a combatant..."

But the "Papay" cut in immediately in obvious anger...

"In the case of Captain Denning... the RUF under my Command has been extremely magnanimous. The High Command of the RUF exceptionally agreed to accord him the full status of a Prisoner of War... otherwise he should ordinarily be treated as a mercenary which is really what he is!"

"Why would you classify him as a mercenary?" The BBC reporter queried.

"Yes... ask him to tell you the Geneva Convention which he likes to recite... What was he doing in the uniform of the armed forces of Sierra Leone? Carrying a service pistol issued by the armed forces of Sierra Leone and receiving mercenary wages from the Republic of Sierra Leone?"

"I take exception to that classification... I have told Mr. Sankoh repeatedly that I am a trainer... working under a Military Co-operation Pact with the government of Sierra Leone... I am an employee of the British Government, who are responsible for my wages..."

"Read your Genera Convention bible!" the RUF leader cut in "You are a mercenary on contract. Yes... you may have probably been paid a salary by your other British employers, I don't care... But you are paid other stipends... home component, oversea bonus, so-called hardship allowance and consultancy fees by the government of Sierra Leone... all amounting to Ten Million Leones per annum... in a country where your equivalent Sierra Leone army Captain earns less than Sixty Thousand Leones per annum... That's the typical description of a mercenary in the Geneva Convention!" Captain Denning was taken aback. The knowledge of his total package in Sierra Leone to the last Leone shocked him... and this bearded, scruffy man with his dumb and unintelligent look... to lecture him on the Geneva Convention on air!

"Is this an interview... some propaganda device or an inquisition?" he asked no one in particular.With no answers to his questions, he continued...

"I reserve the right to remain silent... I am obliged under the Convention to state only my names, rank, date of birth, and serial number; and that's all you will get from me..." At this point, the consummate journalist, veteran war reporter of repute and the authoritative, credible voice of the BBC's Focus on Africa programme saw a major scoop in the making and he pressed on.

"Captain Denning..." Robert Black, older and much more experienced snapped as he cut in.....

"This is a radio interview on the BBC, not an interrogation in a POW camp... I have had to travel in the bush for forty eight hours to confirm to British tax payers that you are alive and well treated... you also owe our millions of listeners an obligation to state your own case and be courteous whilst doing so, even if you don't respect me as a person!" This was shocking to Captain Denning. A British journalist paid by British tax payers to travel all the way to the jungle of Africa to harass and harangue a fellow Briton, who is on an official assignment for the British government!!!. He could not bear it anymore. "Did you say you represent the British Broadcasting Corporation?" He challenged Robert Black, spelling out and emphazing the "British" in British Broadcasting Corporation.

"On whose side are you anyway?" the captain asked the BBC reporter.

"Captain Denning... you cannot lecture me on patriotism and national security. The BBC stands for truth... and I will advise that for the cred-ibility of the British government and the army you represent, you should provide factual answers to clarify your status... are you a mercenary?"

"I will not answer that question"

"Fair enough then... let's move on. Have you been well treated since your capture?"

"I was not captured... I was abducted in Freetown... I have not been well treated as the conditions of living have been generally squalid"

"Foday Sankoh, do you have a response to that?" Robert Black continued.

"Well, if he was expecting the comforts of the Mammy Yoko hotel in Freetown, yes we cannot provide that in the jungle... we are fighting a war you know. However, let me again refer him to his fond Geneva Convention; which says that Prisoners of War shall be quartered under conditions as favourable as those of the forces of the Detaining Power who are billeted in the same area. Now Captain Denning knows for a fact that his living quarters, the food he eats, his medical support, his recreational facilities are excellent; and are infact better than what I enjoy... so what does he want?" Foday Sankoh asked.

"Is that true Captain?" the BBC reporter asked' "Well... you can generally say that would be a fair assessment of the situation... Comparatively speaking... if you consider also the living conditions of the RUF soldiers... but still the conditions are not right"

"Have you been allowed the right of correspondence with your family since your capture?"

"Yes... but I have chosen not to write... I just think it will not serve any purpose... Letters can only exacerbate the current situation..."

"Even to write to your wife?"

"More so my wife... she might just not be able to handle it... she may not believe me... Honestly her understanding was that I was on a strictly training mission in Sierra Leone... so how did I end up being adducted... she could feel betrayed... yet again..." At this point, the soldier in Captain Denning gave way as he sobbed uncontrollably, overtaken by emotions as he thought back to the quarrels, the fights and threats of divorce; accusations of infidelity, betrayals just before departure for his mission in Sierra Leone.

The rest of the interview was fairly routine; almost an anti-climax. Squadron Leader Ikeke and Sergeant Mark Burden confirmed they had been well treated; especially the extra-ordinary medical treatments which had repaired and rectified their fractures. Mark Burden confirmed he was captured in combat on a mission to rescue Captain Denning. Squadron Leader Ikeke said he had nothing against the RUF as his mission was a Recce mission on the NPFL in Liberia. His aircraft had however run into foul weather on his return flight, leading to a crash and his capture.

One week after the BBC radio interview, the three prisoners were marched to the office of the Supreme Commander of the RUF, Corporal

Foday Sankoh. The Papay was in a genial mood as he welcomed them to his office.

"Sit down gentlemen" he warmed them into seats as he re-adjusted his sitting position himself. "I hope you are all comfortable and getting the best of treatment from my people" the Papay continued. "Well" he cleared his throat and announced curtly. "I have observed with dismay the current lack of employment of your training experience and competences. In fact, at a more personal level, I have observed the possible negative effects of your current state of inactivity and resultant boredom... Well, Mr. Denning... you know what you English people say... that an idle man is the devil's workshop. I have therefore decided to keep you people fully occupied. Henceforth, you will be the Commandant of the RUF Officer Training School, right here in this camp" He stopped; and there was absolute silence.

"Nago man" the papay resumed, pointing at Squadron Leader Ikeke, "Nagoman" being the pidgin English Krio fond name for Nigerians.

"Yes... Nagoman, you will be Denning's Deputy Commandant and Mark you will be a Faculty member... After this briefing, Denning will arrange for all the materials and staff support that you require... the first set of officer cadets will be reporting on monday... Any questions?"

"Yes... Corporal" Captain Denning snapped. "May I refer you to article 49 of the Geneva Convention... it says that Officer Prisoners of war may ask for suitable work; but they may in no circumstances be compelled to work..."

"Captain Denning, that is enough!! I will not have more of your distractions... you compound your problems by your poor understanding of the Geneva Convention... You quote aspects out of context. Here..." A visibly angry Corporal Foday Sankoh pulled out a leather bound document out of his side cupboard.

"You think you understand the Geneva Convention? What do you take me for?... I want you to read... yes read the section 49 you refer to...... it says here that the Detaining Power may utilize the labour of prisoners of war who are physically fit, taking into account their age, sex, rank and physical aptitude and with a view particularly to maintaining them in a good state of physical and mental health... so who is correct here" he queried.

Before Captain Denning could think up a response, the Papay continued.

"And to think that you are not even an official prisoner of war, but a bloody mercenary! For a British-trained officer, you are a very poor disciplinary example... You come into my office in a combative mood, refusing to acknowledge and complement me... is that the way you were brought up... not to respect your superior officers?"

"Sir! I will not denigrate the uniform I wear and the rank I carry on these shoulders by saluting a junior officer... a corporal!"

"Enough!! I say enough!! It is purely out of my personal choice that I wear the rank of a Corporal... just to rubbish people like you who carry their ranks on their heads... and think that is all about soldiering... you are a very poor example... Here again... read your Geneva Convention... it says here that Officer Prisoners of War are bound to salute only officers of a higher rank of the Detaining Power; they must, however salute the Camp Commander regardless of his rank" So, do you have another Camp Commander elsewhere that you refuse to pay me proper compliments? Anyway... your officer cadets are here on monday. I want to see your training programme by this weekend"

. "But I don't have my books and course manuals here... "

Corporal Foday Sandoh forced a smile...

"Really?" He pulled open a side drawer and brought out all the training manuals, lecture notes and evaluation exercises that Captain Denning had kept at the Benguema Military Academy, near Freetown. "Are these not your books, personal notes and evaluation reports?... Is this not your field evaluation programme and your tactical assessments? Don't underrate people... that should be lesson number one to you... Never under-estimate the tactical capability of your enemy. Here... you have all the books and manuals you need... so get to work... I want to see your programme this weekend. Good day!!"

The initial results were doubted by the head of the RUF clinic, Captain Bockarie Frazier. He had visited the living quarters of the three prisoners of war to again convince himself that their living conditions supported a healthy lifestyle; that their daily food rations was sufficient in quantity, quality and variety to keep them in good heath; or to prevent loss of weight or the development of nutritional deficiencies; all these in line with the demands of the Geneva Convention. Having established that the prisoners were well-fed, lived in fairly well-appointed accommodation and enjoyed adequate recreation and fresh air, he returned to the clinic and pondered over the case files of the three prisoners: Unexplained weight loss, tuberculosis, chronic diarrhea and now different unexpected skin rashes, carcinoma of the skin and a rash of veneral infections.

In line with relevant provisions of the Geneva Convention, he had organized a monthly medical inspection of the prisoners since their capture and much as he doubted his initial diagnosis, the clinical signs and laboratory results just received, suggested very serious combination of ailments which could only be due to severe immune deficiency. The previous week, he had requested a more independent evaluation of the prisoner's health by inviting the World Health Organization's representative in Abidjan to conduct the tests. The medical inspection of the prisoners had included the checking and recording of the weight of each prisoner, the general state of health, nutrition and cleanliness of prisoners to detect contagious diseases. Blood, urine and stool samples of the prisoners were taken and a comprehensive radiography was done. Now all the results were in; and the medical conclusions were shocking. All three prisoners had compromised immune systems and were all diagnosed to be HIV positive.

The medical review was meant to be brief. But Foday Sankoh insisted on a full case-by-case presentation with the visiting World Health Organization official. Doctor Ralph Bailey of the WHO insisted on the due presentation of an official medical certificate, a copy of which he intended to send to the Central Prisoners of War Agency; in line with the Geneva Convention. But Foday Sankoh was aware of the implication of a prisoner of war suffering from a chronic condition that could exclude recovery despite treatment and how that might become the ground for asking for direct release and repatriation of the prisoners.

"Doctor",he called out quietly, directing his question at the WHO doctor "Have we done all the conclusive tests to ensure that you are not being alarmist? "

"Yes... yes of course... the clinical signs are obvious... and we have done a standard blood test, using an initial assay... the ELISA... and we have since followed up with a more specific blot test... and all three of them returned positive indicators"

"Sir..." the RUF camp doctor cut in "to answer your questions directly.. the test results are all positive for this stage... but where in doubt... there are other tests that we can perform like the oral mucosal trunsudate test, the urine HIV antibody test and others... so it depends..."

"It depends on what?"

"The level of doubt supported by clinical evidence... which in this case is quite low if not absent"

"No... it is not low... They appear healthy to me... they are doing well... training my officer cadets and nothing must disrupt the momentum we have achieved here... so you are going to conduct more tests... and when we are convinced that they have true HIV-positive states, we will treat them here so that they can continue to work here... it will be premature therefore to fill in a medical certificate that will notify the Central Prisoner of War Agency until we are all truly convinced."

"Okay... if you say so... Corporal... but in my experience the clinical signs are obvious... wasting syndrome... tuberculosis, recurrent pneumonia, severe herpes simplex infections, Kaposi sarcoma..."

"Enough! Whether Kaposi... Katanga or Kakata... I don't want to know... I say do a comprehensive test... and then we take it from there!"

For the next two weeks, Doctor Bailey made arrangements with the Abidjan office for test kits and facilities for a more comprehensive testing. When he returned to the RUF camp, he was ready. First, he conducted the Oral Mucosal trunsudate test, using a specially treated pad placed in the prisoner's mouth and gently rubbing between the lower cheek and the gum. The pad collects an oral fluid, the OMT which contains HIV antibodies in an HIV-infected person. He also conducted the urine HIV antibody test, using the urine ELISA and urine Western Blot technique to detect HIV antibodies. Having convinced himself that all the tests returned a positive verdict, he decided to involve Corporal Foday Sankoh on the final Rapid HIV antibody test. Before the test, he educated Corporal Foday Sankoh on the test procedure.

"Corporal... we have analyzed all the results and are convinced that the prisoners are HIV positive... but this final test... you see where in the other tests, you have to wait for two weeks for results, this rapid test will give us results in sixty minutes..."

"Good... so let me see it"

One after the other, the three prisoners were invited to the clinic, their finger tips cleaned with alcohol and pricked with a lancet to get drops of blood. The blood was collected into a vial and mixed with developing solutions. In less than sixty minutes the test device indicated the presence of HIV antibodies in the solutions.

"Good... doctor did you know I used to be a photographer? Yes, I was... so this is like developing pictures from negatives... so I am convinced... so we start treatment today... but first you must manage the way you communicate the information to them so that their morale is not affected negatively... so that they can continue to work while we treat them ...okay...thank you" the Papey instructed.

Doctor Bockarie Frazier had his usual monday morning ward rounds the next day. Thereafter, he had a private session with Captain Denning. "Captain, how are you feeling this morning" he opened on a light-hearted note.

"Fine... fine, considering the circumstances"

"What circumstances, if I may ask"

"Yeah... doctor... considering that I am in confinement... considering... that I am sick. I will say my spirit is high enough..."

"How then would you consider your physical fitness and overall state of health... say, on a scale of one to ten... where would you place yourself?"

"That? Doctor, I would say... I would say three and declining steadily"

"Why is that so?"

"But I just told you... I am not well... and it is getting worse these days... the cough, skin rashes and constant diarrhea is... it's quite bad doctor" "Do you suspect what could be wrong with you?"

"Suspect? Doctor... Suspect ?... I know I have a serious problem... I had known for almost a year now that I was HIV positive!"

"You know?"

"Yes, of course... so when you were going on and on with all kinds of tests... I was truly amused... just waiting whether you would come to the same conclusion... and from your tone of voice and pretended warmth and friendship... I can guess that you and that devious WHO doctor have come to the same conclusion?"

"I am afraid so... Captain... I am afraid so... but why didn't you disclose your status all this while so that we can put you on treatment?"

"Medication?... I threw all of them away just before I travelled to Sierra Leone... They were of no use... making me sick everyday... nausea... vomiting... even eating up by bone marrow... so I stopped them!"

"Did you complain to your doctor?"

"Yes... the prick... wanted more and more money of course for the prescriptions... "

As he spoke, he thought back to why he avoided the Battalion Medical Officer and the NHS to consult the shifty doctor Gupta. He recoiled and stared at Doctor Frazier absent-mindedly.

Born in South Africa to Boer and English parents, he had grown up in Sandton neighborhood near Johannesburg when it was just a small exclusive suburb. Against all advice, he had joined the army officer cadet training, graduated and made steady progress fighting African freedom fighters. But with stepped up terrorist attacks and in the face of mounting international pressure; and when the collapse of apartheid became imminent, he had resigned his commission and relocated to England with his parents. Upon joining the British army, he made progress in Infantry, got promoted, married Sue a pretty country girl from Berkeshire. But Brett always wanted more from the army. Twice, he applied to join the more adventurous and elite Paratroop Regiment and the SAS. After two failures, he put himself forward for selection again. He put himself through a punishing pace of training, climbing the country side hills, carrying weights. But that summer, everything conspired to make him fail.

He had developed sore feet in his pre-training; and when it mattered most during Selection, his sore right foot had let him down as he stumbled and fell down a steep hill and that was the end of Selection. He returned to Hereford disappointed with himself; and sought solace at the Buddha, a popular bar near the Regiment's main entrance. He drank all night; and when it was time to lock up the bar, a busty pretty girl who had made flirtatious overtures at him all night offered to drive him home. It was an initial one- night stand which stretched on to three nights. His return to his Chelsea army barracks flat; and to his wife of six years was uneventful.

But towards Christmas of that year, his pregnant wife had been diagnosed HIV positive and that was when his world started to fall apart. Captain Denning was distraught. A very good son to his very well to do parents, who struck it rich in South Africa, he had looked forward to his first child to cement Sue's eternal happiness. And then, there was the brewing scandal of his wife being HIV positive? His examination of conscience revealed an inner torment, that he might not be entirely free of blame given the grand week- end romp with the total stranger from the Buddha bar in Hereford.

Sue had flung herself at him, punching and crying... her screams rising uncontrollably in crescendo when she returned with the damning verdict from the hospital.

"Brett, you are wicked... God knows I have been faithful to you... God! Why did you do this to me" She had sobbed uncontrollably.

Brett, the ever-loving husband took her into his arms. "Control yourself... Sue what is the problem... I don't even know what you are talking about..." "You bastard... deny it... that you have not been sleeping around... deny it... that you don't know you are HIV positive!! Brett recoiled in genuine shock and fear...

"Me? HIV positive? Impossible... I did my army medicals only three months ago... and I was declared fit as a fiddle... there must be a mistake somewhere... surely, there is a mistake"

"Yes" she retorted "there must be a mistake at your end... with all your army secrets..." He held her close to his chest, stroking her backside.

"Sue... please don't do this to us... there must be an error... and if we have a family problem... let's solve it as a family" With that, Brett convinced Sue that they needed to take some time off; to make a week-end trip to his parents' expansive home at Kingston – Upon – Thames, near Berkshire. In the late hours of a friday, husband and wife got off the train at the ever-sleepy and almost deserted station. They were all alone as they walked down the lonely street, hands held and each in deep thoughts about their future. Their destination was the multi-ter-raced, split level, quiet Victorian house with very large gardens and a long drive-way, adjoining the River Thames.

Pleasantries over, Brett handed Sue over to his mother whilst he sauntered off with his father. They had drinks at the porch of the house over-looking the river, discussed life in London, politics and his impend-ing posting to Freetown, Sierra Leone.

Drinks over, the senior Denning invited his son to join him on his usual evening brisk walk down the main village road, through the vil-lage square, past the train station and back to "Cape Lodge," the father's fond name for his home; a name that brought back fond memories of his time in South Africa. As they walked past the village church, it was the senior Denning who broke the silence.

"What's the problem, Brett... something been on your mind all eve-ning... ?"

When there was no response from Brett he continued... "You are a bad boy... maltreating the missus again... No mail, no telephone... and you just drop in unannounced for the weekend... sure sign of trouble my boy... so what is it?"

An English colonial adventurer in Africa, street-wise. Worldly! With sharp wit and intellect, Denning Senior, had a few signs of ageing in his mid-region and drooping neck and shoulders; but his strides remained firm and agile and his intellect and assertiveness ever – present and irresistible. He turned to his son and demanded an answer..

"Yeah... you are right dad... I have a problem... I am not sure yet... I want Mummy to distract Sue for the weekend whilst I find out... Dad... they diagnosed Sue as HIV-positive at the pre-natal!!"

"HIV? Have you been sleeping around... having unprotected sex? Brett, you can't do that to your wife? What happened to these rubber things... yeah condoms that you young people wear these days?"

"Let's not jump to conclusions yet... dad I said I am not sure yet... I want to do a quick test to confirm... then.... I can take it from there..."

"But why... have you been sleeping around?... What about your marital vows?... Is there a particular woman?"

"No dad... I swear I had been faithful... until three months ago when I flunked the SAS Selection, I had one drink too many... and ended up with this young girl for the weekend... I hardly knew her... just a chance meeting in a bar... even now, I can't remember her name or any other detail... but dad, it was fun while it lasted...."

"Shut up!! You rascal... see what you have brought upon your poor wife?"

That night, Brett and Sue slept in separate rooms in the expansive house; and promptly at dawn, Brett took the train back to London. At the Liverpool Station, he switched to the Underground, taking the District Line to Oxford Circus. His destination was Doctor Gupta's practice on Harley street, a no-questions asked medical clinic very popular with the illegal immigrants and tourist traffic on Oxford street, Tottenham Court Road and Soho. He was eager to maintain strict confidentiality; and avoid getting the results of his visits fed into the NHS and his military records. He presented himself as a South African tourist, paid the standard fifty pounds for registration in an assumed name for the consultation with Doctor Gupta. To be fair, Doctor Gupta was extremely thorough and professional. He stripped Brett of all clothing, examined him physically, checked his nymph nodes, his eyes and tongue;

making copious notes. He then sent him to a diagnostic laboratory down the road for blood, urine tests and gum tests. "Mr. Bortha..." Doctor Gupta had called his assumed name, "some of the results will not be in until next week... but the ones we have here... and the clinical signs I have noted confirm that you are HIV positive!"

"How, why, impossible... I had complete medicals, including HIV test three months ago... and I was clean then... since then I have not had sex with anyone else except my wife..."

"Mr. Bortha... I don't doubt you... or the competence of your South African doctors... but you have to face the facts... now when last did you have unprotected sex with anyone else besides your wife?"

"That should be about three months ago... in fact just about one week before my full medical examination... so you can see why I am so confused"

"No... there is no confusion... the facts are consistent with the way the disease works... Your medical examination, just one week after infection with HIV will not throw up anything. You have to wait for two to three months for full incubation before the test can throw up anything...

At Doctor Gupta's disclosure, Brett collapsed into the chair, sweating...

"Mr. Bortha, take it easy... Fortunately, unlike in the past... there are effective cocktails of medications for dealing with the infection these days.... You see because the disease is so insidious, there is no way of telling by mere look who is carrying the virus. So if you have regular unprotected anal sex... vaginal sex or you share needles then you are just an accident waiting to happen... Especially if your partners are in the acute infection state with a lot of virus in their blood stream; or you have a weakened immune system or you or your partners have open anal or genital sores that get exposed to infected body fluids..."

But Brett was no longer listening... he had drifted far away. Doctor Gupta promptly put him on a cocktail of anti retroviral drugs.

"These drugs will help reduce you viral load... you can live a normal life... but you must avoid repeat infections from unprotected sex and you must maintain the dosage and regimen… otherwise you can develop a resistant strain of HIV that will be difficult to treat."

But the medications were not cheap; and they became a heavy drain on his meager army pay; until thankfully the posting to Sierra Leone came.

With mature counseling from the senior Dennings, Sue was managed through the stressful period. Having accepted her fate, she was more concerned about her unborn child. She was on full NHS – funded treatment when Brett departed for Sierra Leone.

"So have you been taking you medications?" Doctor Frazier asked. The question brought Captain Denning back to the present.

"Yes… I mean I was… even brought enough stock cover from England… but I had problems with the drugs… nausea, vomiting, constant stomach cramps, dizziness and fatigue… these symptoms disappeared when I stopped taking the drugs… so I flushed them away… and was doing well until now"

"I see… I don't know what you were taking before now… but the WHO consultant, Doctor Bailey and I have decided to put you on a cocktail of NNRTIs and protease inhibitors… these classes of drugs work somewhat differently at reducing the amount of viral load… that is the HIV in you blood… we will monitor your progress and review as necessary… all the best Captain".

Squadron Leader Martin Ikeke knew he was HIV positive; and was glad that at last he could come out of the denial phase, share his burden with fellow sufferers and confront the disease with front-line treatment supervised by the WHO.

"My greatest regret" he told Doctor Frazier at the counseling session "was my inability to accept that I was infected... the constant state of denial I put myself... always insisting on my physical fitness... by stretching my physical endurance unduly beyond limits, just to prove a point"

"But did you observe anything untoward before your crash?"

"Yea... I always had what I thought was malaria fever... constant fatigue and dizzy spells..." The dizzy spells had been recurrent in the last three to six months and he had dismissed them off as symptoms of pre and post combat stress.

But it all started at the pre-deployment operational conversion training at the Tactical Air Command in Makurdi, Nigeria. After Basic Air Training School at the 303 Training School in Kaduna, with fixed wing Dorniers, he had done his fighter pilot course on the Alpha jet at the training school in Dusseldorf; and a further advanced fighter pilot course on the MIG-21. He loved the MIG 21 with its delta-mounted wings and easy maneuverability. He had just flown this single engine, single seat supersonic jet into the Kainji Air Force Base after a two-hour routine patrol mission when the Base Commander, Group Captain Akala summoned him for the deployment briefing. The Base Commander confirmed the receipt of a signal deploying him to the ECOMOG Air Task Force. He was to report to the Tactical Air Command in Makurdi for Alpha jet simulator re-training and pre-deployment squadron training before reporting on Operational Rotation to Freetown, Sierra Leone. The pre-rotation training was rigorous as the squadron tore through maps of Sierra Leone, Liberia, Ivory Coast and Guinea. They had air target detection and weapon deployment training; ground attacks sequence in single series and formation, aerial combat engagement tactics, ground strafing, battle group support, surveillance and interdiction and comprehensive ordinance evaluation and deployment. But there was also enough time for fun; and the young female students of the nearby Benue State University were ever ready and willing. The endless parties, the drinking, and the uninhibited group sex were exciting. The raw, unprotected group sex participants were all disdainful of the AIDS campaign as they were all in a denial state as they constantly mocked the campaigns as some western propaganda…

He could not now tell, how, when and who passed on the infection they cynically used to refer to as "American Invention to Deny Sex" to him, given his high number of unprotected sexual escapades with so many different partners. But when he took ill with chronic diarrhea and cough towards the end of the Course, the command's Medical Officer had vaguely hinted at the need to exclude HIV and had planned to recommend him for full laboratory diagnosis, if the symptoms persisted by Martin's next visit to the Air Force Clinic.. Martin never returned for that comprehensive test. Instead, he consulted his friend, kinsman and former classmate, who ran a successful medical practice in the High Level area of Makurdi. There at his friend's clinic where his confidentiality was assured, the chilling revelation of his HIV status was broken to him.

Conscious of his impending annual medical evaluation, which was mandatory for fighter pilots, he had been gripped with nervous anxiety ever since; before his crash and eventual capture.

Mark Burden was unashamedly a Brixton boy. He always saw himself as a born soldier, having been born and raised in the Frontline neighbourhood of Brixton. As a toddler, he lived through all of the race riots, the drugs, the sex and alcohol. By the standards of Brixton, he was a bright, obedient lad that did his parents' biddings. But he could not avoid the peer pressure, the truancy and the three "Ws" of Brixton-wine, women and weed. He started smoking marijuana when he was twelve; and would skip school to sell newspapers and make delivery runs for "Uncle Reggie" just to make some money for the "Three Ws". The senior Burden was fairly comfortable by the standards of Brixton. He had worked all his life with the London Transport, rising through the ranks from driver to Supervisor at the New Cross Station. He had completed mortgage payments on his Brixton flat, and with the massive re-development efforts around the frontline neighbourhood, the flat's purchase value of Forty Thousand Pounds had steadily appreciated and was worth over a Hundred and Fifty Thousand Pounds; and was still appreciating. He was comfortable and provided well for his family.

Young Mark lacked nothing and was pampered with the occasional sunday First Division football at the Highbury grounds of Arsenal. The train-ride, the snacks and drinks that were packed into the sunday treats gave father and son, a very strong bond. Encouraged by his father, Mark was preparing to take his GCS examinations when the senior Burden died suddenly of a heart attack. The death of his father marked a turning point in Mark's life. He turned more and more to the street for support and guidance. The mother, a full-time housewife, who did occasional cleaning jobs at the nearby Marks and Spencer's could not come out of her loss and mourning and constantly shirked her responsibilities in the proper upbringing and the welfare of Mark. That's when "Uncle Reggie" who ran the grocery and newspaper store down the road took over.

"Uncle Reggie" became Mark's best friend, confidant and financier; and eventually his lover.

Mark was fifteen and had been through all the women, wine and weed that Brixton could throw at a growing young man. But always, "Uncle

Reggie" had a special place. It started in those bitter-cold winter evenings. "Uncle Reggie"'s store never adequately heated at the best of times, had had the misfortune of a broken down central heating again that cold winter evening. As he helped to pack and lock up the shop, Mark shivered violently from the cold despite the thick leather jacket that he wore. The "kind" Uncle Reggie held him close and began to stroke his arms, working gently down his bust, stomach and to his back-side. The gentle strokes and massage brought a warm, feeling of longing to Mark. Working slowly but deliberately, the experienced "Uncle Reggie" stroked the now naked body, concentrating on the nipples and the anal region. Then he thrust his tongue into Mark's mouth, working it from end-to-end. In that instant, he gently lubricated Mark's anal passage, turned him around gently and thrust his manhood into him. They went on, two lost souls intertwined and joined together in passion almost like forever... no words spoken, but communicating all the same. It was different for Mark. Different from the things, feelings and emotions he had had with the abundant female stock on offer in Brixton. And to cap a sweet evening, "Uncle Reggie" gave him ten pounds to buy a Rambler pair of jeans trousers that he had always wanted.

It became a regular affair. He dropped out of school and joined a youth football academy at Charlton, but always returning to his lover. Two years later, he joined the army, saw action in Ulster and the Falklands as an infantry man before earning his wings as a paratrooper in the Parachute Regiment. Mark had taken his homosexual habit into the army and had had regular unprotected sex with multiple partners. He had felt unwell for sometime, with frequent bouts of diarrhea, unexplained weight loss, fatigue and chronic anal sores; but had never had a full HIV testing of all three prisoners. Therefore, he was the most shocked and devastated; as he broke down in sobs in Doctor Frazier's clinic.

"You have to control yourself... take it easy... it is not the end of life... you have a chance with modern medication to live a fairly normal life..."

"But how?... oh how? And why me... oh my God... my life is

finished…"

"No… Mark… let's be reasonable" as Doctor Frazier offered him a tissue paper to wipe his tears. "You confirm you have had regular unprotected anal sex with multiple partners… and to be frank with you… that is a very high risk behaviour"

"Really?"

"Yes, of course, some statistics put the risk of HIV transmission via the anal intercourse route as one in ten. Compare that to the claimed statistical probability of one in five hundred for vaginal sex and you will understand your position. Especially as in your case, you are the receptive or what they call the "bottom" partner!"

Seeing that the rational, factual counseling approach was getting the full attention of Mark, Doctor Frazier continued. "You see, Mark let me put it straight to you. Unprotected receptive anal intercourse carries a high risk because the lining of the rectum is very thin… it gets damaged easily during sexual activity… and through it, HIV can enter you body…"

Mark was now frozen in attention like a kindergarten child receiving a lesson.

"Your broken rectal lining… would manifest in pains and blood stains when you pass stools…. and left untreated, the exposed surface of the lining could become a point of entry for HIV and other venereal infections… herpes simplex infections for instance and its recurrent nature will pre-dispose your rectal canal to even more insidious infections like HIV… so now, come to think of it, all that initial diagnosis of hemorrhoids that was made and the suppositories… sheer waste and very misleading. We have to put you on a full HIV treatment right away"

Christmas was celebrated in Sierra Leone that year with so much gusto despite the ravages of the war. Despite the air of foreboding that the RUF south-westerly push could hit the Western province and Freetown at anytime, there was a feeling of resignation. Freetown and its residents were even more carefree and cavalier. To the people of Freetown, Christmas had never been just the one day that marked the birth of the Savior, Jesus. It was traditionally seen as a season, a period, and the whole quarter of the year is dedicated to the celebration of Our Savior. So, Freetown was in celebration from street parades, to moon-light picnics and the London returnees' parties in Lumley and Aberdeen beaches. The war could resume in the second week of January; but sol-diers and civilians alike had thrown caution to the wind to enjoy life that year. To ensure the good life that Christmas, the government had slashed import duties on the main staple,rice and the industrial layout in Wellington was up to the task of supplying the drinks and cigarettes needed for this three-month long party. Earlier in October, the Aureole Tobacco Company (ATC) had launched a new double filtered '555' ciga-rette. Faced with a geographically declining market size as a result of the RUF control of the upland market, Freetown became saturated with '555' and "State Express" promotional girls. Scantily clad in the marine blue brand colours of State Express, their regular bar stormings gen-erated excitement and added colour to the moonlight picnics and the London Returnees' parties. Opposite the Aureol Tobacco Company in the Wellington Industrial Estate, Sierra Leone Brewery had been busy all through the year. Its response to the people's yearning for nourish-ment was the launch of Maltina, an energy-giving food drink, with roots in Nigeria. Using a novel door-to-door sales push with very titivating ladies; and massive sports sponsorships and celebrity endorsements, Maltina became the food-drink of choice overnight. Mixes and remixes of the brand with stout, beer and a local distilled gin – totapak – were rampant. Despite the war, the brand brought an over-whelming crowd of over a hundred thousand spectators to the Siaka Steven's National Stadium to witness the first Inter-Collegiate and Inter – Regional Maltina Athletic Relays.

Freetown was agog with celebrations and parties that year; and Sierra Leone Brewery stepped up its promotional tempo to appropriate the full benefits. Its flagship brand, Star lager beer, the pride of every Sierra Leonian, the Nation's Favourite Beer, launched a promotional blitz with a top prize of a Pajero Jeep and the drinking shifted gear to very high tempo nation-wide. Thanks to the magic of the transistor radio and the Sierra Leone Broadcasting Service, the RUF controlled areas in the provinces fully participated in these promotional offers in Freetown.

As a mark of the undeclared truce during the Christmas, all the RUF combatants were allowed to "dress down". No uniforms, no military fatigues, no caps, helmets and what a kaleidoscopic sight! To the prisoners' astonishment, the RUF combatant ladies whose beauty, poise and vital statistics were hitherto obscured by their over-sized combat uniforms turned out in provocative shapes and attires The Camp 44 week long Christmas celebrations were held at the grotto-like heavily forested quadrangle, with earthly fresh smells of the nearby mangrove swamp and decaying bamboo foliage providing a serene aroma. The men wore assorted makeshift jeans trousers, shirts, boubou robes and funny sunglasses. The nearby markets of Makeni, Bo and Kenema having benefited from the Christmas shopping spree courtesy of the special RUF Christmas bonus to all combatants, the assortment of clothes, fashion styles and steps knew no bound for the Christmas. The three prisoners' allowances were used for the procurement of elaborate cotton and brocade Makeni-style long shirts, with matching caps; and they looked gorgeous as they regaled themselves in the celebrations. Sure enough, everyone arriving the Quadrangle wore a new dress befitting of the occasion.

Abenaa had chosen a simple pure Dutch wax "Hollandis" which had been made into a smart blouse and a wrapper by the RUF tailors. The blouse was designed with smart side hemming to accentuate her very firm and provocative frontal cleavage. With her soft, sure-footed walk and proudly erect carriage, she was the cynosure of attention as she walked in and took a seat near the prisoners.

There was more than enough to eat and drink. Jollof rice, fried rice, white rice and stew, coconut rice and payela rice. The ubiquitous Star lager beer, Guinness stout, the newly launched Maltina from Sierra Leone Brewery and Totapak were in free supply. With the free-flowing drinks and food, all inhibitions were set aside, as a wild party ensued;

with the Papay's nod of approval. Seated at a high chair on an outcrop, he took all the details in, with amusement and visible joy. After dinner, the women found ready company and the serious dancing began. The Sahara Band, the fond name of the makeshift RUF band, drawn from former professional musicians captured the mood aptly and switched gear to a high tempo Congolese Kanda Bongoman rendition. The crowd responded in ecstasy.

Towards midnight, as the celebrations reached a crescendo, a high -pitch scream ripped above all the music and rapturous noise; as every man and woman in the Quadrangle looked in the directions of the high excitement. The source was one of Corporal Foday Sankoh's six-foot tall P.G.s (Personal Guards). Libyan-trained and extremely loyal and quietly efficient; he was not one to shout and display excited emotions. He approached the Papay animatedly showing him a piece of a Star lager beer crown cork.

Soon, the news was all over the Quadrangle; and the master of ceremony; with fever-pitch exuberance made it public.

"Ladies and Gentlemen... My Papay... With Maximum Respect Sir... All Una... ; I say E'Kushe, Kushe... Ekushe!"

Having secured the attention of the tumultous crowd, he continued: "Tonight... I say tonight... even the gods have smiled on our endeavours... the gods of Salone have tonight endorsed our struggle... Tonight... the missing rib has been found!"

Silence: Absolute silence: He then continued:

"For over three months... Star Lager Beer... The Nation's Favourite Beer... God's Gift to man... Shine – Shine – Bobo has been running a consumer promotion... And the Star prize? The Star prize Ladies and Gentlemen.... A Pajero Jeep!"

Silence. More deafening silence.

"Tonight" he continued "I say tonight, the Pajero Jeep... with Four Wheel Drive... With Power Steering... With Air – conditioning... has been won... I say... has been won... by Corporal Lonsanna Conteh!

At an elaborate ceremony at the picturesque headquarters of Sierra Leone Breweries in Freetown in January of the following year, the Pajero Jeep, long mounted for promotional display in front of the brewery was driven down the apron. The event, covered live on the state radio had senior serving government officials in attendance. An excited Felix Button, the British Managing Director of the brewery made a speech extolling the strong bond of friendship between the brewery and the people of Sierra Leone; and especially between Star Lager beer and its teeming loyal consumers. He emphasised that despite the civil war in the country, Star lager beer's core values and proposition of Brightness and Friendship remained even more relevant; and that the Star promotion had created a unique platform for the demonstration of friendship; sharing and brightness across the war – torn country.

The combatants of the RUF gathered around transistor radios around Camp 44 listened to the speeches and presentation ceremonies with rapt attention; and the prophetic undertones; ironies and symbolism of Mr. Button's speech elicited back-slapping, laughter and jeers. The climax was the hand-over of the winning Star lager beer crown cork, with the Pejero Jeep specially embossed with gold trimmings on the inner layer of the crown under the plastisol. A certain Mohammed Kamara from the junction town of Masiaka, the owner of the crown cork and thereby... the winner of the Pajero beamed with smiles as he posed for photographs with dignitaries; and an elated Felix Button. Finally, the long-awaited point arrived; and in a symbolic hand-over of the winning crown cork from Mohammed Kamara to Felix Button; and a simultaneous hand-over of the keys and documents to the Pajero by the Managing Director. There were drum rolls; cymbals and confettis as the crowd burst into a spontaneous applause.

The "We Papa – Girls Rhythm Band" burst into a pulsating rendition of "Freetown Baby... You Give Me Chest-Pain..." and the dancing, drinking and celebrations commenced.

Speaking to reporters later, Mohammed Kamara said he was overwhelmed by the warmth, friendship and the sheer display of integrity by the brewery. That ordinarily, he was not given to gambling and never really believed in raffle draws and promotions, but that he thought differently after winning the Star prize. That his journey to stardom started in Bo, where he bought drinks from Mammy Nancy Nichols Store for his child's birthday ceremonies. The rest, he said, was now history. That same evening, Mohammed Kamara accompanied by friends took possession of, and drove the Pajero all the way through government controlled towns of Masiaka, Mile 91 and Bo. That night, on an unused earth road between Bo and Magburuka, the Pajero veered into a bush path and disappeared.

For Abenaa, the work of providing medical care for the combatants and prisoners filled her with fulfillment. To stitch and scrub wounds; to straighten fractures and dislocations; to inject and administer prescriptions and deploy her nimble, delicate hands assisting in the theatre gave her immense joy and power. All she had learnt from her father and all the medical training received from the MSF doctors provided composite competences that she deployed with so much pride and self-assurance. She saw and carried herself as an elite medical attendant with the gift of life in her hands. Knowing that she had touched the lives of all her patients was joy enough, but the respect and virtual adoration was overwhelming. Now and again, she would look at the hand-held mirror in the makeshift bathroom and marvel at the wonders of nature. How she had been moulded into a full grown woman. She would cause her hands to probe her full, ripe breast, her flat, inviting tummy, and her romantically dewy eyes, mounted on her beautifully sculptured oval face.

She would raise her arm and straighten the creases on her dark eyebrows and brush inviting little oil drops from her firm, narrow nasal bridge; and agree with herself that she was beautiful.

It was now over nine months that her beloved Captain Mondei departed for the Course in Libya. Every morning in the last two weeks, she would put on her pretty white uniform, ensuring the accentuation of all her curves, powdered her face nicely and anticipated the excitement of her husband's return. With evening would come the disappointment of another day and the endless wait for at least a letter from her beloved. It was not just his intellect, charm and warm jovial manners; of late, she had felt a certain longing in her bosom and loins that she could hardly suppress. Even in her dreams. Nostalgic flashes of what was truly nature's best gift to the two of them. How could he have been so carried away on this Course in Libya that he never bothered to write, she would wonder. All of these loneliness and empty nights and to watch for animated sensuality each passing night and not a word from her loved one? Much as she had hated the loneliness and the sight of being visibly alone all through those Christmas celebrations, at least the excitement of the crowd and the obvious feeling of being admired provided some comfort and assurance. From anger at him for not writing; and remorse for being unnecessarily angry at a man who was probably going through a grueling period on a Course in Libya; she resigned herself to her poor fate. It did not matter that she had many admirers. Infact the lecherous stares and inviting glances were most times rude and provocative.

But the tall, handsome Nigerian pilot was different. The first time she had seen him, Abenaa could not take her eyes off the young man writhing in pains as she plunged the syringe deep down his veins. Abenaa was not an unduly emotional woman. She had been betrayed and defiled by one man and rejected by her heartless ultra traditionalist community... and yet now felt rescued and loved by one man. The one and only man in her life whose overdue return from Libya was beginning to be a source of concern. But standing over this Nigerian fighter pilot, with her stethoscope, syringe and other medicaments, she felt totally captivated. This was not what she had often been told of the typical Nigerian man. They were supposed to be brash, loud, arrogant and selfish ,greedy, of doubtful integrity and conceited. But this pilot was classically handsome with a ready, gentle smile and a cute moustache. Ever so polite, he conveyed a certain inner strength of character, he had a warm and friendly disposition, and a compelling charm that spoke more than words could have.

The sheer force of his personality was enchanting and she felt deeply aroused and stirred anytime she touched his supple skin during treatment. She therefore worked hard to consciously avoid him to suppress her desires and protect her marital vows... !

She was scrubbing his backside that evening, preparatory to administering an injection; and she could not hold back her interest:

"I found you very quiet and subdued all through the Christmas celebrations" said Abenaa. She was blushing uncontrollably and she barely managed to hold her hand steady as she administered the injection. In her job, she had seen every part of the male anatomy; but outside of her strict work relationship, she was quite unfamiliar with men in a sensual flirting sense. She was a pretty girl in every material particular; and lecherous men endlessly made overtures to her; but she had a shy natural upbringing and always avoided making eye contact with men to protect herself.

"So you noticed? I thought you were too busy being admired to notice... anyway... what is there to celebrate?"

"Why, don't say that" picking on the theme of celebration and tactfully avoiding the discussion of her admiration. "We have to celebrate life... everyday of it that we are gifted by the Almighty to see... He makes the day and the night... He giveth and taketh life... Therefore, we should be grateful to Him for keeping us alive..."

"Yea... for keeping us alive in subjugation and sickness... I have seen better days... for which I was duly grateful... but this?... this life... is this life?"

He stopped as abruptly as he started, controlling himself.

"I am very sorry I aroused your anger... just believe that the Lord works in mysterious ways... He will work his miracle... you will see... just have faith and believe in Him..."

With Squadron Leader Ikeke maintaining a stoic silence, Abenaa quietly slipped out of the room.

Then the ferocious rainy season came. As the rain pelted the camp, day in, day out, Abenaa dreamt of what could have been. How the cold nights would have prompted the warmth of his man's flesh on hers for the planting of seeds that would nourish a future generation. Night after night in the squalid little apartment she shared with her batman, she dreamt repeatedly of their previous innocent and unrestrained love making and how he would cup her firm breast in his hands and milk them, fondle them and suck them, and whisper things to her to calm her anxiety about the war.

"Forget about the war... you worry too much... just think about us together like this always and you, will not have problems... be positive okay?" He would then lead her stage-by-stage as he made love to her... gently initially... and gradually building up to a strong forceful crescendo, with mutual joy and satisfaction.

The Papay walked down the long passage towards his office down into the cave. With his characteristic shuffle, his Personal Guards running ahead of him to clear the way in double time. There was an instant wave of excitement around the camp as the news of his return spread round the camp. The news that the "Papay" had returned from his tour of the frontline towns of Sefadu, Matotoka and the meeting with ECOWAS leaders in Accra. The Papay watched, waved and broke into a confident smile as he acknowledged the shouts of "Papay... Papay..." Abenaa beckoned to her ADC and asked.

"Since the Papay has just returned from Accra... you think he might have information about my husband... ?"

"Why... don't you go and ask him now that he has just returned... you may never have this opportunity once he settles down and gets busy".

Without further prompting, Abenaa ran down the quiet corridor; suddenly overtaken by emotions. When she got to the lower level where the Papay's office was situated, she held her breath as she was accosted by Foday Sankoh's stern-looking Personal Guards. The Papay looked up from his table far into the room hardly visible and barked an order.

"Let her in!"

She walked into his presence and saw that he held in his hands a sheaf of papers and many unopened envelopes. Perhaps one of the envelopes could be a letter for her, she thought. He looked up with a broad smile.

"How good of your to visit my office!"

"Papay... welcome sir! Just thought I should come and say welcome... and to enquire whether you heard from my husband during your trip to Accra?"

"Thank you very much... after such a long trip... I thank you for the pleasure of your company... and for bringing your concerns directly to me... thank you"

"Thank you sir... but is there any news?.

"Please sit down" As Abenaa took the offered seat, the Papay got up, walked over to the window and turned to face her with the sun playing up his silhouette.

"Is there anything you lack... anything so that we can provide all your needs in the absence of your husband?" She was too shy to answer directly... she blushed and turned sideways.

"No Sir,... I am quite comfortable... considering we are in a war situation".

"Good... I want you to know that I quite understand how deeply you love your husband."

"I do Sir," Abenaa replied shyly.

"Good... I don't want your current situation and the absence of your husband to interfere with the depth of love you have for him. Your husband is a dedicated and loyal officer whose exemplary performance at the course so impressed the Libyans... they have accepted him on another Course which will run for nine months"

Abenaa heaved a sigh of relief.

"But Sir... at least he should write!"

"Yes that is true... but you know these bloody Americans... they have imposed an embargo on everything... and even letters from Libya to loved ones are being confiscated. Just be rest assured that your husband is well and has you in his thoughts wherever he is... always!"

After that they exchanged banters and he politely escorted her to the end of the corridor where she bade her goodnight.

A sense of sadness and foreboding had enveloped the camp that weekend. In whispers, discussions were held in little groups about the disastrous military failure and heavy losses on Mile 91. As the sullen stillness and quiet was occasionally broken by the noisy flights of hawks and crows overhead, the prisoners did their best at teaching the RUF cadets despite their failing health. Through a small slit in the window in her room, Abenaa peered through to take in the emaciating figure of Martin walking back from the Officer Cadet School area. She stared in disbelief as he walked unsteadily, looking so thin, a shadow of his former self, drained of his colour, vitality and had become sallow. Martin walked up to a heavily sand-bagged anti-aircraft emplacement and rested his steadily depreciating frame against the sand-bags.

Suddenly, she turned from peering and turned from the window and walked towards the kitchen to prepare a meal; but primarily to occupy herself and take her mind away from unfaithful thoughts. She looked around the kitchen. There was nothing she lacked; but she had this feeling of alienation from the pleasures of her accommodation and excruciating feelings of unease, unhappiness and general emptiness. She had never felt this kind of longing before. She had made her husband's favourite cassava leaves soup; and as she stirred the sauce, she felt lost, strange and weak without his warmth and looming physical presence: What's her husband doing?... Treating her as if she did not exist, not writing, she wondered. What could he be doing and thinking in Libya now, she thought. Could he also be thinking of her or carried away by the attraction of some Arab damsel? She wished she knew. She wanted her husband back, as she felt lost and empty without him. She served the cassava leaves soup into a plate and as she carried it from the kitchen stove to a table, she looked through the window and saw Ikeke again; this time walking slowly to his living quarters.

As she looked more intently into the impartial mirror in her room, she saw staring at her a young girl of extreme beauty; with a dark chocolate skin, bright sexy eyes and an ornately crafted; royal and regal face. She swung the mirror to take in her full, firm and provocative breasts and she could see her throbbing nipples responding to her menstrual period in elegant fullness. Her body parts manifested the un-spoilt life she had led and the near total preservation of her chastity. That's how she had preserved herself and like true wine, had matured in taste, flavour and sensory values. Now difficult to suppress, even in her immaculate nursing white uniform, the prowling eyes and the many who swallowed saliva in passionate thoughts at the sight of Abenna around Camp 44 could be forgiven.

Whilst those with suppressed passions were many; the more direct Nigerian prisoner of war, the tall, elegant fighter pilot unburdened his interest and flirtatious intent quite early.

"You are so distant and dispassionate to us prisoners... why? Why won't you take lunch with me for instance?" Martin Ikeke had asked... a question which caught Abenaa off-guard. Whilst she fumbled for an appropriate response, she struggled to avoid his romantic probing gaze as she came up with what she thought was an eventual smart response.

"We... girls... we eat together in my quarters... so they will miss me... besides I don't want to starve you of your full meal entitlement..."

"No... it is not just about the food... I am talking about our common humanity... the warmth in sharing things socially... even now this discussion... just talking to you... it has done a lot of things to me... it is a wonderful therapy... please... would you talk to me... more often... please!"

Abenaa did not provide an answer and stormed out of the room awkwardly. But since that day, over five months ago, he had filled her mind; she had watched his every single step, when he drilled the officer cadets in ceremonial march, when he looked so dignified and intellectual in carriage in his lectures; when she felt totally captivated by his charm and arresting presence....

Martin would tease her repeatedly anytime she had to administer his treatment.

"I am Squadron Leader Martin Ikeke... I am a Nigerian Air Force fighter pilot... Prisoner of War number 20213455... please remember me in your prayers... and if by chance you are in contact with the outside world, please mention where, when and how you saw me..."

"Ah, so you want me to tell them to come and rescue you and take you away from me... ah! You can't be serious!!" She would tease in return.

Abenaa always carried these encounters back into the loneliness and emptiness of her room. She would always fantasise about the first opportunity she had to administer an injection on his buttocks. How the silky feel of his skin against her fingers sent unimaginable sensations through her body. But always at the height of her fantasies, she would be drawn back and reminded of that very solemn ceremony with Mondei in Gbarnga:

"You have willingly undertaken to contract marriage... a holy sacrament ordained by God... It is a precious sight in the eyes of the Almighty... This union of two very young and attractive bodies have found grace in the sight of the Lord and the Lord will bless you with children, He will provide all your earthly and heavenly desires and you should share your love in laughter and happiness forever and ever and until death do you part..." She would recoil and break out in sweat. On those occasions, she would seek solace in reading her bible for spiritual re-armament and for the Lord's wish to be done in her marriage.

Squadron Leader Martin Ikeke, his hair newly cut in a severe skin shave looked straight into the class at no one in particular. Despite his frail, emaciated frame, he looked elegant in uniform and his speech was motivational. The students were all seated on makeshift benches in the makeshift classroom. His fellow faculty members, Denning and Burden were also seated on reserved benches at the rear of the class taking in the entire lecture. Captain Denning looked on intensely wearing a permanent look of curiosity at the very in-depth treatment of the topic: Wars in West Africa: Political Motives. Martin had traced the origins of wars in; and the collapse of the ancient Kanem-Bornu, Songhai, Mali, Benin, Oyo,Ghana and other empires for proper perspectives and dwelt extensively on the political motives for modern wars in Nigeria (Biafra), Liberia, Sierra Leone and the festering crisis in Ivory Coast. He concluded that apart from the purely economic scramble for a fairer share of the national wealth, usually borne out of the corrupt enrichment by the political class, the mass perception of marginalization,

nepotism and inequity; the political foundations of the countries as created by the British and French colonial administrations after the Berlin
Conference for the Partition of Africa was the single most contributory
causal factor for civil wars in West Africa. After the lecture, the prisoners walked slowly along the footpath that led to their living quarters.
Captain Denning was first to break the silence as they walked.

"You know... Martin, you Nigerians surprise me... Here you are...
just a Squadron Leader... but intensely patriotic and intelligent. Your
deep insight and intellect always comfounds me... why a country like
Nigeria so blessed with intelligent people like you will always produce
very, very dull, unintelligent misfits as leaders... Yes not just in your
politics... but also in your military leadership"

"There you go again... wild generalizations... do you have any evidence to support these your assertions?"

"Yes... why not? The paucity of political leadership is all too glaring...
corruption, nepotism and the sit-tight leadership syndrome... fragrant
disrespect for term limits and constitutions... and your superior officers... I have dealt with so many of them who are half... as intelligent
as yourself and yet.. they are supposed to be your superiors!"

"Well... blame that on your people... That's like going back to the
lecture to the students. The British ran Nigeria, including the Nigerian
Military until 1960... The officers you referred to are products of the
British ineptitude and political meddling in the evolution of the Nigerian
armed forces..."

"There you go again! When will you people start taking responsibility for your failings as a people and as nation... After all the British left
your country so many decades ago... look at your June 12 elections...
you say it was free and fair... but look at what happened. It was annulled
just like that..."

"And what have the British done to challenge the annulment as a concerned former colonial master... who created the problem in the first
place?"Martin retorted.

"What should the British have done"

"A lot... I say a lot" Martin stopped abruptly, brought out a map of

West Africa and spread it on the ground.

"See... the ancient empires of West Africa were created along horizontal culturally contiguous lines... so people with similar culture, religion, ethnic background were grouped together and lived happily with each other... But your people went to a conference in Berlin and partitioned the continent vertically by just looking at maps... very unmindful of cultural affinity... and that's the basis for most of the conflicts in the sub-region... Look at this map... all across the North of West Africa... you have Muslim, Hausa/Fulani, Wollofs, Kanuri,Madingos... whether in Nigeria, Republic of Benin, Togo, Ghana, Ivory Coast, Sierra Leone,Guinea or Burkina-Faso... same dress forms, same architecture... The same in the South: Christians of Yoruba, Edo, Igbo and Ashanti stock. But in your cartographic Berlin arrangement, greed and hurry, you forget these basic principles... and you blame us for the resultant bickering?"

"No. Tolerance, that's what you lack. Intolerance of each other, lack of nationalism and unity..."

"No... That's a simplistic approach. Didn't the same British administer colonial India?

And on the eve of India's independence... despite the protestations from the two great Indian nationalist leaders Ghandi and Nehru,the British advised that Hindu India and Muslim India could not survive as one nation? And that's how Pakistan was created. And the little chunk of Muslim remnants in India-Kashmir... has there ever been peace there? What of your own country? Since your potato inspired crisis in Ireland... and the Catholic – Protestant divide... have you ever known peace in that country?... So you have to put these crises in West Africa into proper context..."

"Martin! You always surprise me! I am sure your High Commissioner in Freetown... even your Foreign Minister would not have these your unique insights... Honesty, I don't agree with your positions... but at least I respect your point of view..You are perfectly entitled to your opinions."

They argued animatedly all the way to the Quadrangle where an evening programme was in the offing. As they made to sit down, loud cries of "Papay, Papei" ran through the clearing. It was the sort of wild adoration that Corporal Foday Sankoh had come to expect anytime he made a public appearance. A few hours before, he had been on tour of the frontline areas, sharing meals with the troops and giving pep talks to keep up the morale of the fighting forces. From all corners of the Quadrangle, excited crowd of enthusiastic supporters hung out, some from the adjoining tree-tops crying emotionally at the return of the "Papay." All around the "Papay," were his specially trained Personal Guards(PGs), led by the tall, tough-looking Sergeant Simon "Cobra" Collier, who looking beyond the crowd held up his arms in a smart salute.

The "Papay" had just returned from Sefadu, on a day of crowd adoration in the diamond mining town. With impressive traditional dances and the rich cuisine for which the gold mining town was fabled. But rumours had travelled back to Camp 44 that it was a trip filled with anxiety and trepidation; as Intelligence reports had warned of a planned synchronized attack by government forces backed by Nigerian ECOMOG soldiers and air support to decapitate the RUF leadership. With his triumphant return therefore, it became obvious to the crowd that the "Papay" had given a lie to the threat; thereby proving his invincibility yet again.

Soon enough,the assassination attempt on the Papey in Sefadu which gave rise to the widespread rumour of his death began to filter in.The reports indicated that in the Papey's usual casual, friendly manner, he had decided to take a stroll down the city of Sefadu after a review of the troops and tactical discussions with senior military personnel on that front. There was a tumultuous crowd of well-wishers every where. They thronged the streets in ecstasy to behold the sight of the invincible "Papay." But amid the laughter and back-slapping, an elderly man of not less than seventy, who was later to be identified as the former projectionist at the popular Opera Cinema broke through the security cordon, shouting something about the murderous regime of the RUF and how he had lost two generations of his children and grand-children to the RUF invasion. The "Papay" had hardly listened to the accusations above the tumultuous roar; and only had a moment to look up before the old man brought out the rest of his frame from out of the crowd and the gun in his hidden arm. Sergeant "Cobra", with astonishing reflexes rammed his frame against the "Papay" and brought the RUF leader down in a rugby tackle. The "Papay" had a sense of something flashing past his left ear and saw that a bullet had smashed into the bulky frame of the town's Garrison Commander who was standing shoulder-to-shoulder with the him earlier; a second bullet narrowly missed the "Papay's" head, just ripping through his fabled Temne hat and the ceremonial feather patched on the side.

In a flash, the old man was wrestled, tackled and brought down in a torrent of fists, kicked legs, drawn daggers and blows; and was pummeled into submission. It was all over in a twinkle of an eye. The "Papay" was held up and he beckoned on "Cobra" and the rest of the group to continue with the walk round the city. The city tour concluded, he rode through the town triumphantly and disappeared into the jungle and thence to Camp 44.

With the events of Sefadu earlier in the day put behind him, the "Papay" settled into a high seat and waved his hands for the show to commence. It was Easter Monday and beyond the Christian significance of the day; it was an opportunity to encourage socialization and the morale of his fighting forces. In scene after scene of gaily dressed units in traditional folklore dances reminiscent of the WASA – an army traditional social assembly created by the British for the West African Frontier Forces; and long since adopted by armies in West Africa after independence. The sight was hilarious and highly entertaining... the sight of tested fighting forces in funny clothes and caricatures was soothing to the war-weary nerves.

Then came the climax of the evening entertainment – the "domei". This intricate narrative drama of the Mende people; a favourite of the "Papay", which had served him well in the past to release tension and to speak in parables. Whilst the performance in the hand of an elderly adept leader would have depth and intellectual under-pinnings; the Camp 44 performance had a strong emphasis on riddles, conflicts, dilemmas, proverbs, coded folk communication and fairly tales.

"Tjatjala!" The young combatant shouted; and the crowd responded in unison.

"Behold, this beautiful girl... a very beautiful girl... Long, Long ago...."

"Which beautiful girl... it is a lie... you are too ugly to have even seen a beautiful girl... !!" The crowd responded sarcastically.

"Ah! It is not me... O! I could not have had the courage to behold such a majestic beauty... !" And the crowd burst into a general laughter.

"This girl... so beautiful... when she is going to the stream, a thousand men would hide in the bushes to catch a glimpse of her beauty!"

"A thousand men... I am sure you are telling lies again!"

"No! even the king... when he heard of the beauty... came down himself to ask for her hand in marriage"..."

"Hey! Were you there?"

"Yes... even Corporal Bundu here... he was there! The girl snubbed the king..."

"Heh! a whole King!"

"Even the richest politician in the land... he said all he wanted was just a chance to cuddle her rich breasts... and he would die a happy man... and he too was denied!"

"What of me... would she marry me?" A voice from the rear shouted.

"You?? With your knocked knees and oblong head?" "Then... the Kakaaki War broke out... A powerful enemy general heard of the famed beauty... and invaded the town to capture her"

"Did he marry her?"

"No way... The proud girl refused his hand in marriage... so the general locked her up in solitary confinement and went to war... One year..."

"No... Two years!"

"Three years!"

"No Six years!"

"Twelve years!"

"No... Twenty-four Years!"

"Forty-Eight years!"

"No Fifty Years! And the general kept fighting wars in far away places... and the pretty girl... like a beautiful flower began to wither... I say she began to wither".

"Wither?"

"She began to wither"

"Wither?"

"She withered and withered and became very old and ugly".

"And she lost all her charms and attractiveness and went into menopause and in desperation... she started crying....."

"General... General come and marry me!"

"Me? A General..marry an old hag?"

"My Dear King.... Please let me join your harem" "Really?"

"My Dear general... don't even marry me... just come and make me pregnant!"

"Pregnancy at menopause!"

"Oh! My Dear King... please, please, please let me

have a child for you... just one child to make me a complete woman...."

So the guards at the prison heard her cry repeatedly every night... and they took pity on her... and made love to her repeatedly... Every night..."

"Every night?"

"Yes... and even every afternoon..."

"Heh! Twice a day... ?"

"Who said twice... Three times a day... for breakfast for lunch and for dinner but it was too late for her to make babies!"

"What a calamity!"

"It is terribly my people... the last time I went to Kpando... the once beautiful girl was now very old and ugly... and was now a common prostitute..."

"A prostitute?"

"Yes – o! And who would touch an old prostitute... when there are those sweet young-young ones who will make a volcano out of any mountain?... and that was what I heard long ago!!"

And thus with music, call and response songs, the "domei" brought the evening's programme to a close. But the lesson and moral were clearly obvious: Make hay whilst the sun is still shining... don't be proud, haughty or selective for the tide waits for no one.

The Captain swung the horse to the right so that he brushed through the hillside in one fast gallop. Then he saw the lion. Unusually frightened by the sight of the mounted horse, the lion took flight, with his mane thrown backwards in a fast gallop. Surprisingly, the horse was not frightened or intimidated as it drove forward in graceful speed as dust, smoke and sweat filled the air; with the horses' hooves on the hard ground. The horse was gaining on the now very frightened lion as the smell of death filled the air. But the lion made desperate strides, digging into the ground to rake up dirt and dust, some of which stung Captain Denning's eyes. He struggled to maintain control whilst wiping the dirt off his eyes. But the mounted horse seemingly on auto pilot maintained course in hot pursuit as Captain Denning crouched forward and gripped the rifle in readiness for a clean shot. Then he loosed a new surge of speed on the horse that almost brought him to talking distance with the lion. So close, he looked amazingly so attractive. In its awesome, gracefulness his shaggy mane looked pleated in a peculiar African hairstyle of the Ki-Swahili people that he had seen at the Kilimanjaro-Randolph Lodge the night before. The lion looked desperately frightened as his eyes darted sideways to take in the horse and its mounted hunter. The lion's eyes looked bloody as it shot out its tongue in frightened salivation that streamed backwards to hit the Captain in full face.

Now, the horse was galloping heroically, matching stride for stride as it drew level with the lion. Captain Denning dropped the reins and gripped the .303 Remington rifle to take aim. As he did, the big horse felt triumphant and burst forward. At that instant, the lion looked at him and steered off in a fast swivel to a fast about turn. Captain Denning felt the horse twist and shift to take the new course of pursuit and it stumbled on bumpy ground that hit and twisted its right hoof awkwardly. A loud cry of agony escaped from the suffering horse as it groaned and stuttered to an abrupt halt. As it struggled to accommodate the weight of the rider despite the pains of its dislocated hoof, both horse and rider looked up to see the lion, now sensing an opportunity for a kill bearing down. The horse in deep fright panicked threw its arms frantically high, and instantly flung Captain Denning from the saddle as he pitched forward violently and fell. Captain Denny pitched and fell head-long, lunging and rolling, with his eyes ringing, bright phosphorous lights flashing through his head………. and when he came to and looked up half a dozen claws thundered by to pelt his bare flesh as the giant teeth of the lion closed in for a final kill……

Captain Denning woke up in sweat and chilly spasms, glad that it was only a nightmare. But the chill and sweat continued unabated. He attempted to open his mouth but it was so dry, he could not open it. A painful grunt escaped his lips as he made to shout for help. He could hardly breathe and every attempt to move his limbs felt like tons of bricks had been heaped on them. A constant pressure build-up and ringing in his ears made him feel deaf… but he could barely hear the distant barking of a wild dog in the adjoining hills as he passed out………

Squadron Leader Martin Ikeke felt a lump tighten like a vice grip around his throat. Of late he had had problems swallowing. The shortness of breath was explained off as a possible reaction to the cocktail of drugs. He had lost weight quite appreciably and an endless cough made horrors of his nights. As he gasped for breath that night, he heard two owls in the distant hills overlooking the Camp whispering to each other in very low conspiratorial tones. He strained to listen for any hidden symbolism, but the more he strained his ears, the more distant the conversation of the owls.

It was the period of the endless rains, thunderstorms and whirlwinds in Sierra Leone. The rain had poured non-stop for three days and three nights; and stopped on the fourth day as abruptly as it had started. The dark clouds had given way to a cool, clear night. Now, two owls were whispering to each other in this cool clear night and the Nigerian fighter pilot felt a heavy thud on his heart with every distant whisper of the owls. From the distance, he heard a sudden flutter and a muffled shrill squealing of the two owls. He thought he heard his name called… and responded with a jerk. He strained and listened intently and it was the two owls in deep squealing that were mimicking human sound... and calling his name?

He was sweating intensely now. He stared intently into the thick rain forest for any hidden signs. He kept his eyes trained into the dark jungle... waiting... watching... and he heard the owls whisper his name again. This time in a dry, thin shrill. This time, the shock hit him like a thunder-bolt. It was too much to bear... his throat convulsed violently as it narrowed abruptly. As he struggled, there was a mental stirring of fear, apprehension and anxiety all mixed; and a peaceful resignation to the inevitable. He gave up the struggle. The futile resistance to the general debility that was gnawing away at his throat and entrails..... one last bloody cough and he collapsed in a quiet whisper into the cold rocky floor.

The two owls, members of "strigidae" family of nocturnal birds had a particularly notorious superstitious deathly association with most West African natives. Associated with evil and bad omen, their for-ward-piercing eyes and flattened faces had an awkward ugliness that frightened the natives of this sub-region. Because of their soft, fluffy plumage, they easily flew noiselessly and had a way of sneaking into human households. Concealed all through the day, they came alive at night to fly around and prey on insects and suck human blood accord-ing to West African myths. The natives of Sierra Leone believed that the owls only flew at night when they had sucked enough human blood and were fulfilled. Therefore, to allow an owl suck human blood and fly back into the forest portended danger. Little wonder then that when just before dawn, Doctor Frazier was woken up to the presence of the two owls fluffing their wings around his room; his anxiety knew no end, despite his western medical education. He struggled in futility to kill the two owls in his room. In hot pursuit, he chased them down the long cavernous corridor to the living quarters of the prisoners of war. There, the owls flew into the room shared by the three prisoners of war. Now joined by a battery of duty guards and driven by the superstitious beliefs of his people, Doctor Frazier chased the two owls to the ground and had them killed. But in all the pandemonium that ensued during the chase and eventual killing of the two owls, not a single movement came from the three prisoners of war.

With the two owls killed, the experienced medical eyes of Doctor Frazier turned to the prisoners and he quickly sensed there was a problem. He checked their pulse readings and he was alarmed and how barely audible they were. The eye lids revealed that he had an emergency. Quickly, he arranged for the three prisoners to be wheeled to the Intensive Care Room of his clinic and notified the Papay immediately. They were quickly put on intravenous sterile saline solutions for prompt rehydration. By mid-day; and with the condition of the patients deteriorating, he risked the administration of a steroidal injection to act as a catalyst in the activation of key organs and vital signs.

It was probably too late or too sudden for Mark Burden. With a prolonged cough and a violent shudder, he stretched his frame fully and gave up the struggle. A quiet smile appeared on his handsome, youthful face as he slept peacefully in death. There was now absolute panic around Camp 44 at this unforeseen development. With the blood pressures of the two surviving prisoners plummeting to very dangerous levels, there were frantic suggestions to commence immediate ambulance evacuation to the more fully equipped NPFL Field Hospital in Gbarnga. But Doctor Frazier ruled that option as a no go as the tortuous twelve-hour journey through narrow foot-paths would surely kill the prisoners en-route. A journey to the Tongo diamond field airstrip for onward medical evacuation on an air ambullance to Abidjan was also ruled out on grounds of security.

Meanwhile, with the intense tropical heat and the ever-present tropical flies, Mark's body was already showing signs of deterioration only a mere six hours after death. Promptly, in accordance with Article 120 of the Geneva Convention, Doctor Frazier had to abandon the treatment of the two surviving prisoners to concentrate on a full autopsy for the purpose of a Death Certificate to show the identity, date/place of death and causes (s) of death of the prisoner, for on- forwarding to the Prisoner of War Information Bureau. The Doctor worked all through the day, taking the organs one after the other for critical examination. The primary cause of death was established as the failure of the liver,and subdequently the heart arising from HIV treatment induced complications. In discussing his report the next morning with the Papay, before forwarding same to the Prisoner of War Information Bureau, the shocked RUF leader could not understand how, despite the best of WHO medical care, the prisoner could die from HIV-related complications just like that. It was an over-worked Doctor Frazier who had to explain issues of drug resistance and drug failure, mutations and toxins to Foday Sankoh, who listened all through like a child.

"Sir! The patients are on three different medications taken in combination to manage their HIV-induced immune defficiencies. Additionally, I have had to recommend medication to treat any reported opportunistic infections. The drug interaction with the body processes and with other drugs can affect the body negatively".Doctor Frazier reported at his briefing to the Papey the next morning.

"Medically", he continued, "we talk about what a drug does to the body and what the body does to the drug... and any of these interactions could lead to death.."

"But why the three of them at the same time... and how come we didn't know of this earlier?"the Papey queried sharply,in obvious anger.

"We knew. The WHO representative and I have had the situation under close monitoring and a scrutiny of the prisoners medical trends in the last three months... viral loads had been growing instead of declining... liver damage as a result of viral hepatitis and increased opportunistic infections were observed and reported... the last two weeks had been bad... more infections, pronounced weakness and loss of muscle power... all of these traceable to drug interactions"

"But the prisoners were better before the commencement of. all these your drugs and treatment" the RUF leader cut in.

"Well... they may have looked better on the outside... but the HIV load was building up inside of them... and I must say also sir,.... that they created problems for themselves by their stop-go usage of prescribed drugs... leading to severe mutations of their original infections... I have discussed this with the WHO expert. When the viral load kept rising in the patients despite their medication, we jointly agreed to change the combination therapy following the initial treatment failure... But even the new combination was not helpful because of mutations induced by non-adherence to medical prescriptions previously... We had planned a review for next week... and now we have this problem."

"Huh!!" It was not a sigh and it was not a question or exclamation. Just a reflex... an involuntary exhalation of air. But it said a lot about the stress and the state of anxiety of the Papey as he thought about options available to him in the management of the prisoners of war medical crisis.

With a motley band of a full musical section; and the RUF, Sierra Leone and the Union Jack flags flying at half mast at Camp 44, Sergeant Mark Burden was buried in a very solemn ceremony. In accordance with Article 120 of the Geneva Convention, Mark's hand-written Will and the Death Certificate indicating place, cause and time of death were sent through the WHO representative to the Prisoner of War Central Agency and the Prisoner of War Information Bureau. Captain Brett Denning and Squadron Leader Martin Ikeke, who had barely come out of coma, were wheeled to the graveside to pay their last respects. Captain Denning being the closest, nearest relative and by virtue of his service rank performed the dust to dust ceremony. The 'Papay' read a glowing tribute about valour, gallantry and his respect for all co-combatants, friend or foe fighting for whatever causes they believed in. As the coffin was lowered into the grave, filled and covered with sand; the solemn occasion was marked with a long, moving trumpet blast; as everyone stood to attention to salute the fallen British paratrooper.

"Don't throw the book at me... I hate when people pass the buck unnecessarily!" It was the 'Papay' in a very combative mood, presiding over a medical review meeting with his Medical Officer and the visiting WHO representative Doctor Bailey. The WHO representative had in accordance with Article 109 of the Geneva Convention requested for the urgent evacuation of the two surviving prisoners, first to Ivory-coast and subsequently to their home countries on the grounds that the two prisoners were "incurably sick according to medical opinion... their mental and physical fitness seemed to have been gravely diminished... and.... they are not likely to recover within one year and.... their treatments required urgent very advanced technological intervention beyond what was available at Camp 44"

"Listen, my young man... you are as culpable as anyone else for the disaster we are trying to manage... so don't talk about Conventions here... let me take you through the contradiction in your request"The Papey paused for rapt attention and continued.

"Article 30 says prisoners suffering from serious disease or whose condition necessitates special treatment must be admitted for special medical care; even if future repatriation is contemplated..... We have done that and infact you have been part of the medical team..."

"But the patients have not had access to modern diagnostic..."

"Let me finish!" the Papay snapped.

"Your Article 31 says medical inspection of Prisoners of War shall be held at least once a month. We have done that with your full participation; and you personally prescribed the medications that endangered the lives of the prisoners..."

"No! I take exception to that statement. The medications did not endanger their lives... the lack of initial care, the abandonment of treatment initially and identified cross-resistance caused their HIV mutations... Now the two survivors have developed wild mutant strains of the infections that require very advanced, specific laboratory diagnosis... The amount of HIV in their blood or what we call viral load has been increasing instead of decreasing... their immune system is now dangerously compromised exposing them to opportunistic infections that can kill them. Their CD4 cell count is so dangerously low that they can die from even the commonest cold right now... is that what you want? The two patients now have chronic hepatitis B infection, with consequent fibrosis and cirrhosis of the liver... What this means is that their livers even now lack the ability to process their drug intake because of their impairment. In their condition, death is imminent... so we must act, right now."Doctor Bailey pleaded.

"You listen to me..I say listen!"Foday Sankoh snapped back in anger.

"You don't scare me with all your medical jingoism... what if they die? Do you know how many of my loyal soldiers fall in battle every day? And here we are talking of enemy combatants who chose to kill us in the first instance. Mr. W.H.O.... May I now refer you to Article 47 of the Geneva Convention? It says sick or wounded prisoners of war shall not be transferred as long as their recovery may be endangered by the journey... are you prepared to take responsibility for the grueling thirty-six hour bumpy ride through very dangerous combat terrains and poor roads to take the prisoners to Ivory Coast?" Silence. The silence from the WHO representative was deafening... and thus ended the medical review meeting and discussion on possible evacuation or repatriation of the prisoners.

Martin Ikeke sat in front of the room starring straight at the make-shift altar. A bottle of holy water, freshly blessed by Father Cardogan was beside him. From the other end of the room across the wide entrance door, the church choir struck a sorrowful dirge; and gradually worked the small congregation of family members into frenzied tears. When the choir switched to and Bellowed:

"When the roll is called up yonder... shall you be there?," the throng of sinners and unbelievers around the room shifted uneasily in discomfort. A mourner in an all black designer outfit came over to Martin's side, bent over his shoulder and whispered...

"My son, I thought you were one of the regular alter boys... why... you are not assisting Father with the mass today?"

"No ma... I served at the Vigil mass with Father and assisted with the blessing of the holy water here..." She recognized the bottle from the Sanctuary that holds the holy water and her eyes lit up instantly....

"You must tell the Father... he must bless me with the holy water... and you must conclude the Anointing Sacrament... quickly, now" She said hysterically.

"Why... this is an important sacrament... you are shouting and distracting the congregation" Martin said.

"I don't care... you must leave now... I must get my jewels, my money... my foreign exchange and the secret bank accounts in Switzerland... he gave them to me freely... he loved me..."

"Who are you talking about, madam?"Martin asked. The mourner turned sharply, pointing at the weary old man, slumped on a sofa at the head of the room; the subject of the Anointing Sacrament.

"My husband... he loved me. But his children and relations all of them never do wells... they hate me... they despise me as a whore who is just after the Old Man's money... he is dying now and I am at their mercy... help me"

As she shouted, she clasped her hands around Martin's throat in a suffocating grip whilst reaching for the bottle of holy water at the same time.

Oblivious of Martin's struggle for life in a corner of the house, Reverend Father Cardogan continued with the anointing service; beginning the rite with the sign of the cross, with blessed water as a reminder of the baptismal promise to die with Christ so that we might rise to a new life with him. The Sacrament of the Word then centered on the transience of materials and material life and the eternal joy and glory of spiritual salvation and the life of bliss in heaven for those who will be called to the Lord's banquet. Father Cardogan then imposed his hands on the head of the dying man; he then prayed over oil and anointed his forehead and hands. Silently, he prayed for the salvation of the dying and invited all present to pray The Lord's Prayer. Holy Communion was given; and finally the Father blessed all present; especially the sick for protection against untimely death and for the will of the Almighty to be done in their lives. The choir stuck a recessional hymn and the priest, led by the alter boys left the house, followed by the entire congregation. Suddenly, the entire house was now empty. Martin, Father Cardogan's off-duty alter boy in his white cassock with the red trimmings now ruffled, was alone with the lady in black struggling for his life. As the lady tightened her vice-like grip around his throat, he felt life ebbing out of him. His flailing arms tried to call for help. With his vocal chords cut off, his grunts and cries were hardly audible.

From the side of his eyes, he saw that the old man, who was the subject of the anointing service, whose sins had just been forgiven to prepare him for heaven in the ceremony of Anointing Sacrament had risen up from near dead and was bearing down on Martin and the dark lady in a menacing manner. Threatened by this development, the lady's attention was diverted, just for a moment. Martin used that instant to reach for the holy water which he sprayed aggressively at the combined threats from the man and the lady in black. As he sprayed them, he shouted…

"Jesus, Jesus" repeatedly and the two-some evaporated in a grey smoke. He continued to shout "Jesus… Jesus" as he broke out of the terrible nightmare in sweat; to see Abenaa holding his hands and wiping sweat off his brows. Instinctively, he grabbed and held on to Abenaa for protection "A-B" he called her fondly, "Thank God… you are here… I am dying… I need to see a priest… Please, get me a Catholic reverend father… I need to be anointed before I die…"

"Why… you will not die… you have gone through a lot… but the difficult period is over… all the same… I will get you a priest as requested…"

There were just a handful of worshippers at the makeshift church at Camp 44. Besides Squadron Leader Martin Ikeke, Captain Brett Denning also elected to participate in the anointing sacrament. The Medical Officer, Abenaa and a few orderlies and batmen completed the congregation. The Chaplain, a prominent peace-time priest of the catholic church in Kenema presided over the special mass. The Chaplain thanked Brett and Martin for their faith in Jesus and belief in His Holy Catholic Church in this, their very trying period. He said the special mass of the Sacrament of Anointing provided a unique opportunity to remind practicing Catholics of their Creed; and to correct the erroneous impression that the Anointing Sacrament was for the terminally ill at home or in a hospital beds receiving a final ritual of forgiveness for the final preparation for heaven. The Chaplain emphasized that the Anointing Sacrament was not only for those at the point of death but for anyone who was seriously ill, including mental and spiritual illness. That tensions, fear and anxiety resulting from the war and general insecurity affected not only the body but the mind as well. The physical and psychological outcomes induced by security anxieties, he said, could result in hypertension, heart ailments, ulcers, mental illness and dementia.

That as true children of God and true Catholic baptised and confirmed in the faith, the congregation should not wait until their illnesses became so grave that the Sacrament will have to be celebrated on a death bed. That was why; he said the Anointing Sacrament was a community celebration and should be preferably celebrated in the context of the family and the parish before going to hospital. He then said special opening prayers for Brett and Martin for their anointing, speedy recovery and the guardianship of the Father, the Son and the Holy Spirit. Then followed the First and Second Readings from the healing miracles of Jesus from the Book of Luke and the Homily which provided another opportunity for the Chaplain to stress the healing powers of our Lord Jesus for those who worship Him and truly believed in Him.

The two sick prisoners were then wheeled to the altar; where the Chaplain laid his hands on their heads. He recalled Jesus' own usual' manner of healing by quoting extensively from the Book of Luke 4:40... "....at sunset, all who had people sick with various diseases brought them to him. He laid his hands on each of them...."

Oil was then brought to the altar and the Chaplain said prayers over it; and made the Sign of the Cross on the sick prisoners' forehead whilst saying... "Through this Holy Anointing... may the Lord in his love and mercy help you with the grace of the Holy Spirit"

. The chaplain took the hands of the sick prisoners in turn to anoint their palms with the Sign of the Cross whilst saying...

"May the Lord who frees you from sin save you and raise you up..."

The special Anointing Sacrament continued with bread and wine on the table for the Eucharistic Sacrament as the mass continued.

The next morning, dawn broke on Camp 44 without Abenaa. Accompanied by her batman and two heavily armed orderlies, she had sneaked out of camp; with the full permission from the Papay to scour the country side for herbal remedies. She was out for a whole day and returned with loads of plant stems, roots, leaves and barks. She was particularly happy with the discovery of a water-borne reed that grew rarely into a full tree on the banks of tropical swamps. That night she relived the scene in the Papay's office which gave her the new mandate to try her hands on the prisoner's treatment.

All through the discussion between the Medical Officer, Doctor Frazier and the 'Papay' the previous morning, she had maintained a studied silence. Doctor Frazier had explained that following the HIV treatment failure, the next natural move would be to undertake a full investigation of why the drugs failed through a Resistance Test. He explained that the Resistance Test would indicate why the treatment and the HIV virus had become resistant to one or more medications. With the continuing rise in the viral load of the patients and clear evidence of treatment failure, a Resistance Test had become inevitable, Doctor Frazier said.

Unfortunately he said, the facilities for such advanced Resistance Testing were not available locally.

"So, what are you proposing?" The Papay queried. "It is difficult Sir... knowing and sharing your strategic vision on the issue... I cannot now be seen to be proposing the very route recommended by the WHO representative... which you have already rejected..."

"You and your WHO people! Where were they... when life threatening fractures were treated by our sister here... Where were they?"

Turning full face to Abenaa, the Papey asked her directly...

"Have we explored herbal and alternative traditional options... we don't have a choice in the matter now... For over nine months, you people have relied on the white man's medicine... supplied directly by the WHO... and we have seen the results in one dead and two dying!! Is that what we want...? Abenaa can you help?" Abenaa was silent for over five long and agonizing minutes....

Finally in response, Abenaa had asked for a free hand and total exclusion of orthodox medical applications in the course of her treatment. She explained that there would be definite adverse effects arising from drug interactions if the two streams of treatments were allowed simultaneously. Adverse reactions ranging from spontaneous bleeding and interaction with anticoagulants and antiplatelet agents, cardiovascular events, seizures and death. Due to the more direct effects of traditional herbal applications, their increased direct potency after very limited administration could trigger untoward interactions with underlying residual impurities from orthodox medications like allergens, pollens and spores from the inability of the liver and kidneys to excrete the toxins.

Abenaa was promptly given a free hand by the 'Papay' with Doctor Frazier nodding in agreement. She commenced by regenerating the livers and kidneys of the two patients damaged through months of different anti-retroviral medications. Every morning before the first cockcrow; the two patients were required to chew and swallow six nuts of bitter kola (garcinea kola) and drink two glasses of bitter leaf water (venonia amydalina) on an empty stomach. Abenaa explained that the nuts and bitter leaf water would revive their livers to full function and dislodge the hepatitis B infection and cirrhosis; and generally clear all toxins from their system. For good measure, she put them on coconut water (cocas nucifera) which they were required to drink freely as an elixir, health tonic, cleanser and a remedy for all the accumulated poisons in their blood stream. She maintained this regimen for two weeks to achieve total detoxification and revitalization of the liver and kidney and watched for another two weeks for the patient's vital signs and the natural reaction of their immune system.

At the end of one month, Abenaa moved the patients to the HIV treatment phase. In the one month of waiting, the very important stem of the aquatic reed had been dried into a sinewy stick. She cut the sticks into smaller one-foot portions and asked the two patients to chew freely, like the way West Africans chew a variety of chewing sticks to clean their teeth. But in their case however, Brett and Martin were required to swallow their saliva and the roughage from the stick as they chewed.

In addition, Abenaa put some of the dried reeds in a large earthen pot and put them to boil just for thirty minutes. The boiled reeds turned the water into a dark red syrup. When cooled, she administered two, small beer bottles before breakfast and dinner every day. In less than two months, the appetite of the prisoners became very healthy and Abenaa ensured a steady supply of rich fruits and vegetables. By the third month, the scabies-like skin rashes on the two prisoners, earlier diagnosed as a form of kaposi sarcoma had cleared and the chronic tuberculosis which caused their sleepless nights, coughing and choking had all disappeared. In six months, both patients had resumed normal activity; their full strength back again. After six months without a recurrence of Brett's chronic painful and severe herpes infections, he became even more hopeful of a permanent cure. The wasting syndrome which characterized their physical appearance; with the rapid weight loss which accompanied the onset of the disease disappeared. With smooth glistening skins, the more robust, fleshy and muscular patients now took part in the physical training and tactical maneuvers of their officer cadets.

But Abenaa insisted on the continuation of their medication to avoid any relapse. She explained that their reported incidents of frequent urination was good and therapeutic as it helped with the elimination of toxins and all remnants of the HIV virus in their blood steams.

In line with Article 31 of the Geneva Convention, the RUF Medical Officer Doctor Frazier had dutifully organized proper medical inspections of the prisoners once a month; with appropriate medical reports made for the records of the Central Prisoner of War Agency. Since the boycott of these monthly medical inspections by the Abidjan based WHO representative, Doctor Bailey following his disagreement with the RUF leadership, all hope had been lost on the possibility of the prisoners' recovery. But month after month since he stormed out of the meeting with Corporal Foday Sankoh, the reports from Camp 44 had been positive on the steady recovery of the prisoners under a new regimen of so-called Traditional and Alternative Medicine "TAM" as Doctor Frazier regularly referred to Abenaa's methods in his Medical Inspection Reports.

Intrigued by these Reports, Doctor Bailey arranged for a visit through the usual circuitous routes of Abidjan in Ivory Coast and Gbarga in Liberia and eventually to Camp 44 in November. He was pleasantly surprised at the physical presentation of the patients. At the cadet officer training recreation area he played long games of squash and volleyball with the two patients; whilst covertly assessing their physical strength. Satisfied with what he saw, he proceeded with detailed clinical tests the next morning. Doctor Bailey reasoned that HIV and AIDS were difficult to evaluate exclusively with physical examination; but could only be established or ruled out through proper clinical diagnosis. Only a full diagnosis could establish that the patient's CD4 count had dropped below 200 cells/mm3.

He therefore came prepared; and put the two patients through a comprehensive testing programme – Standard blood test, oral mucosal transudate test, urine HIV anti body test and Rapid HIV anti-body tests. The results were incredible. The HIV in the blood of the two patients had disappeared. The life threatening viral load of his last visit had given way; and was now totally undetectable. The CD4 cells in the two patients had grown enormously and their immune systems had fully recovered to start doing their protective job again in their bodies. So elated was Doctor Bailey with their recovery, he broke away from Doctor Frazier and Corporal Foday Sankoh to embrace the two prisoners.

"This is incredible... it is nothing short of a miracle."

"Yes... Doctor... Captain Denning concurred "a miracle of the Almighty

Himself... but of course, God works through people... and I am personally so indebted and grateful to Abenaa for this miracle..."

But Doctor Bailey would not concede easily and give credit to Abenaa.

"Captain... we have to wait and see... You see HIV is a very tricky infection... even when you think it is eliminated, it could be hiding in the genetic structure of many cells in the body, in hidden reservoirs such as lymph nodes and spinal fluids where medication can hardly touch it... so we are not really sure it is over... until it is actually over!"

"It is over! I don't agree with your pessimistic view... and you should be open – minded enough to accept that we have made progress since the last time you saw us... and that somebody has been responsible for that progress..."Martin Ikeke lashed out at Dr.Bailey. There was a spontaneous applause led by Corporal Foday Sankoh himself and with Doctor Frazier and Captain Denning clapping and smiling in excitement.

"Well spoken Martin... very well spoken... 'Nagoman'....some people see only what they want to see, you know".Foday Sankoh said.

And with that anti-climax, the medical review meeting ended abruptly.

"I don't want you to get me wrong" Doctor Bailey said the next morning to Abenaa before his departure to Abidjan. "I very much appreciate what you have done with your God-given talent. I have a very simple request... can you give me the set of herbs, stems and the methods that you used... I want to do a pharmacodynamics and pharmacokinetics analysis of them, so that I will let you have the results during my next visit"

"You know... Doctor... even my personal batman and orderly who provided the security cover during the search for my herbs and plants were crucially kept away from seeing what I went for... I kept them over five kilometers away... and I came back to them with my herbs hidden in a large duffel bag... that is the way of traditional medicine... that is the way my father taught me this skill... that's our own form of patent and trade mark registration...that's how we protect our intellectual properties... so you see Doctor... you can't have anything from me for your analysis... but of course you can analyse the results... please feel free to take as much blood samples as you want from the patients... do your analysis as many times as you like with the samples... and write your reports! Good day, Doctor!"

Abenaa made to walk out on Doctor Bailey but he held her back pleading with genuine interest in his eyes.

"Do you understand what this means? If we could validate your methods, the effective constituents of your drugs and the scientific proof of your cure... do you know you could become the richest woman on earth?"

"Doctor... you are British or American... anyway it doesn't matter, you are all the same... you do not understand the ways of Africa... Our traditional healing powers are a gift from the Almighty... The Almighty ensures that every African clan is gifted with the divine powers to heal... and these powers given for free must be used for the good of mankind. The traditional African healing must be for free for it to be efficacious. I will lose my divine gift to heal the day I commercialized my healing powers... I am also enjoined to protect the secrecy of my healing herbs and methods because they are for me only... and never to be shared. The day I share my methods, my ancestors will strike me and all my loved ones with an incurable pestilence... that's what my father told me!"

"And you actually believe that utter rubbish?"

"Yes, of course, that's the way of my people".

The Briefing Room was on the HMS Niger-Delta for the assembled elite SAS unit. There were large relief maps of Sierra Leone and the adjoining countries of Guinea and Liberia. There was a general air of hushed urgency around the room as the men of 'F' Squadron of the SAS filed in. People smoked away nervously as if their lives depended on the cigarettes as they waited in anxious anticipation. The Squadron had been flown first to the aircraft carrier HMS Waterloo, the flagship of the Flotilla; where they had been in waiting for the last two weeks. In typical Navy tradition, everything about the room was clinical: white paints, white, clean table cloth, even the projectors on the table looked new, efficient and of course white. A table of biscuits, sandwiches, tea coffee and orange juice was laid to the right end corner of the room and the men had a go at the snacks freely as they waited.

Suddenly, there was a momentary agitation and a hushed unease descended on the room as the Commanding Officer walked in. His style was to shock the unit.

"Gentlemen, listen to this"... and he ordered the Tascam tape recorder in the corner of the room to be played. A loud trumpet and an underlying blend of percussion, the signature tune of the BBC Focus On Africa Programme was followed by.

"This is Dan Stapleton of the BBC Africa Service... Over eighteen months ago, Brett Denning, a Captain of the Parachute Regiment of the British Army was abducted in Freetown, Sierra Leone... and deep in the jungles of Sierra Leone our Focus On Africa reporter Chris Black caught up with him in this shocking interview...... ....

Black: Over eighteen months in captivity and still no sign of release... do you feel let down by your country?

Denning: Let down? No, not at all... Mark you there have been attempts to rescue me... but all of them failures due to probably wrong intelligence and sheer lack of professional competence!

Black: So what do you expect next from your country? Is a prisoner exchange or repatriation on medical grounds being considered?

Denning: I don't expect anything. I am fit as a fiddle... I have been well looked after by the RUF... honestly I feel more committed now more than ever before to our common humanity... as members of one large, global family. If we all shared that philosophy, we will have a world without wars...

Black: So, do you regret your involvement in the war in Sierra Leone then?

Denning: Yes, of course. First, Britain has no business getting involved and fueling the crisis in the first place... What was I doing in Sierra Leone? I was training and arming one side to the conflict in Sierra Leone on behalf of the British Government... I am not sure the British tax payer would accept that.... Why don't we use our colonial influence and authority to broker peace instead of instigating wars?

Black: So you agree with the RUF claim that you are a British mercenary?

Denning: There is nothing to disagree with in that claim... if you

take the technical definition of the term "mercenary" yes I was a mercenary... I was paid... do I say my total emoluments were far, far higher
than what my equivalent in the Sierra Leone army received... and I was
a foreign combatant in a general sense, since I contributed to the Sierra
Leonian war effort.

Black: Do you look forward to your eventual release?

Denning: No. Why should I. I was thrust into an unjust role in Sierra
Leone... Captured and abandoned by those who sent me here... I was
a very sick man before my capture... Today due to the care and dedication of the RUF... and here I must pay special tributes to the innova-
tive methods of a gifted nursing personnel, Sister Abenaa... you can
see yourself that I have been well looked after... so I don't really look
forward to my eventual release with any enthusiasm.

Black: And your wife and family?

Denning: My sincere apologies to them for my views... I am sure they
will understand."

At a signal the tape recorder was switched off and there was dead
silence in the room.

The Intelligence Officer took over at this point of the briefing.

"Gentlemen... these things happen! The Doctors say it is a sign of
nervous breakdown and extreme gratitudinal bias. We have seen that
happen in Vietnam... with American prisoners of war declaring alle-
giance to the Vietcong cause. In the case of Captain Denning, we have
fresh reports coming in that he was actually diagnosed to be HIV-positive before his deployment to Sierra Leone..."

There was a shuffling of feet and whispers of shock as the squadron
was struck like a thunderbolt by this new piece of information.

"Well... gentlemen... if I can have your attention... that he was HIV
positive is not the news. The news is that in the course of his incarceration, a certain traditional healer took him into her personal care, treated
him and reportedly finally cured him and reversed his HIV status!"

The room was suddenly thrown into muffled laughters and back slap-
ping. But it was Sergeant Tommy Todd, the 6" 2" mean-looking man-

machine at the rear of the room who broke the silence... "Now... that is something... if we can get our hands on this traditional healer... we will all be rich... boys... this is it!" This was followed by excitement and general laughter.

The Commanding Officer cut in curtly to restore control.

"No, that is not it... following the BBC report, Whitehall and the MOD have come under very severe pressure. We understand that the BBC is planning a follow-up report which might be even more embarrassing. Your task therefore is to locate and abduct Captain Denning. I say "abduct"... because he may not be willing to return to his unit and England. If he refuses to come with you, you have to assume that he has declared himself AWOL; then you must neutralize him and bring him back to face desertion charges. Let me repeat the Tasking Statement: Locate and bring back Captain Denning. The Intelligence Officer will take over from here... Richard."

"Gentlemen... your area of operation is around the two hundred miles of thick mangrove and rain forest with the following co-ordinates" as he flipped open a large relief map of Sierra Leone.

"This here" pointing to a series of hills surrounded by jungle.." was the last location of Captain Denning. The RUF in Sierra Leone, a rag-tag army operates in this jungle and have many garrisons here... The most prominent being Camps Eleven, Twenty-two and Forty-four. Our man is believed to be in Camp Forty-Four... here!" The I.O. paused to take a glass of water and continued.

"In view of our last experience... and because our man may be unwilling to return, we are avoiding a frontal attack... Instead, only six of you will be going in with Puma attack helicopters.The rest of the Squadron will be billeted here(striking a point on the map) and will be maintaining Jump-Off positions to provide tactical support as necessary. Your drop zone is marked on your maps... all the maps you need... information on altitude and possible sources of fresh water supply and main enemy footpaths,supply lines, ,altitudes,rivers and mountains are in your folder. The duration of your task will be eight days and the Situation Room will be in radio contact all the time... your call sign will be DeepQuest.

Any questions?"

"Yes sir!" Sergeant Doug Beasley shouted from the rear

"What is the temperature like over there, what is the weather forecast for the area for the next one week and the location and disposition of any friendly forces"

"Thanks Doug... this is the rainy season in Sierra Leone... and a lot of rainfall is forecast... this is good from a tactical point of view in terms of water supply, camouflage, rehydration and stealth. The enemy is seldom active during the heavy rains... it means you can strike when you have the element of surprise on your side... the positions of friendly forces are clearly marked on the maps with you... Now here... Your special weapon for this mission...... this weapon fires morphine based tranquilizers. It is effective at fifty meters... if you have to use it... you must not fire more than two bullets on any one target to avoid overdose and possible complications. Good luck."

As they flew by Chinook off the Atlantic Coast line into Sierra Leone, Sergeant Doug Beasley looked past the wing gunner into the vast Atlantic void. They were flying very low into the drop-off point to avoid enemy radar and reduce the aircraft's visual profile to anti-aircraft batteries. The need for operational secrecy was stressed repeatedly during the briefing and the fact that friendly forces were very nearby in Sierra Leone and Guinea made the operation seem light weight, but you never know, he thought. The element of surprise was crucial to the mission's success. Quiet entry and a very quiet exit would be in line with the mission commander's expectation. They had agreed the drop-off point to be close to the lying up areas which was at the foot of the Jojoba hills, with thick enough foliage for concealment. The patrol would commence systematic tabbing from there, bearing all its entire requirements. Apart from the Universal Purpose machine gun and explosives, all the other weapons had silencers. The patrol also carried enough ammunition, food, drinking water medical kits, compasses and the all-important radio communication. There were two hand-held back-up radios to the main unit carried by the signals man.

Doug looked across the Chinook and found the other five members of the patrol sleeping? Or perhaps in deep thoughts with their eyes closed. He could not sleep because his mind was racing and analyzing all the possible angles and obstacles as the Patrol Commander.

They flew north-easterly, just before dusk. The pilot had decided on the pre-dusk timing for operational security with a strong argument that day-time environmental noise would mask the Chinook's rotor noise. Despite the squadron's preference for a night drop using night vision equipment, the tactical surprise element would have been lost with a noisy rotor noise since it was generally agreed that rotor noise travelled very far at night. The Chinook continued on very low level tactical flight and Doug could see some fishermen on dug-out canoes as they flew past the coastline into the Sierra Leone mangrove forest.

Just before take-off, Doug had assembled the Patrol for a Final Orders Briefing. He again explained the political history of Sierra Leone and the reasons for the conflict and Captain Denning's role in the conflict. He repeated the Intelligence report on the state, disposition and morale of the RUF and its enigmatic leader Corporal Foday Sankoh and his Libyan training background; his close ties with the NPFL in Liberia. He highlighted the main areas to be covered during the Patrol's eight days of tabbing; the maps of the area stressing altitude, topography, relief and all existing roads and foot-paths which serve as supply lines to the RUF. Doug was sharp and dramatic about the mission statement when he repeated it. That this was not just anybody or someone else. That Captain Denning was one of their own who must be rescued and saved from himself in the overall interest of the army and Great Britain. Sitting at his corner of the Chinook, he thought back to his dramatization of the mission statement. He is one of us... an officer and gentlemen of the British Army... a paratrooper who worked hard to earn his wings... a gallant officer who saw action in the Falklands and Iraq... so whatever they did to him... whatever they put in his head for him to sound the way he did on that BBC programme....."

What did they put in his head? He thought, as his mind wondered again to the mission commander's briefing and the BBC's Focus on Africa interview...

BBC (Black): You appear happy in captivity?

Denning: Let's just say I am not unhappy... that my captivity has afforded me a unique opportunity for self examination, deep reflection and a much more dispassionate and objective assessment of the conflict in Sierra Leone:

BBC: Captain Denning, perhaps you would like to share some of your perspectives?

Denning: Why not? I believe that these African conflicts are avoidable if the British government did not provide tacit support for the exploitative tendencies of multi-national firms involved in diamond mining here. The British government as a former colonial master has a duty to encourage and support the rights of the people of Sierra Leone for the realization of their social and economic rights and for the full enjoyment of their God-given diamond resources; and in the interest of national unity and equity...

BBC (Cutting in) But how is your support for the policies of Corporal Foday Sankoh helping to effect these changes?.

Captain Denning (Abruptly) Don't get me wrong. I am not and will never be a supporter of Foday Sankoh; not with all the atrocities committed in his name... but I believe that he is just a pawn, a victim of multinational diamond politics in all kinds of unholy alliances with the government of Sierra Leone and the British government on the one hand and the NPFL on the other.

BBC: The British government?

Denning: C'mmon don't be naive! When was the last time the British government pushed for enforcement of environmental impact assessments before their companies or any other company for that matter carried out diamond mining in Sierra Leone? Let me tell you, these diamond mining companies are extremely powerful, technologically advanced and very rich... richer than most countries in Africa. They have frequently used their financial, political and diplomatic influence to foster a mutually rewarding political and economic relationship between the corrupt, puppet governments of Africa and themselves to the exclusion of the people; especially the diamond – producing communities.

BBC: Captain Denning, these are very weighty allegations... do you have proofs, perhaps some documents to support your position.

Denning: What proof? Have you ever visited the diamond producing communities of this country? Go... and take a look at how the whole land has been excavated and polluted and how the communities have been left without farmlands, the high poverty level, poor housing and disease... and how the privileged employees of the multinational diamond corporations... most of them expatriates use financial inducements and enticements to turn the young maidens of these diamond – producing communities to sex slaves and sex workers... the degradation and deprivation of these communities end up in fat multi-national profits, taxes to the British government and numbered Swiss accounts for the corrupt African politicians... is it so difficult to see this relationship that you, an investigative journalist should be asking me for proofs?

BBC: So how do all of these justify the RUF, its bestiality and your continuing incarceration?

Denning: Well... I am also a victim... a pawn sent by the British government into this festering conflict... It is the unhealthy relationship between diamond mining multi-nationals; the failed expectations and social frustrations arising from the poverty of the host communities vis-à-vis the conspicuous and ostentatious lifestyles of corrupt politicians and corrupt multi-nationals that has produced the endemic culture of aggression that gave birth to the RUF. Can't you see... ? The RUF is just a symptom... even if you eliminate the RUF and Foday today, there will be more RUFs tomorrow unless you tackle the root causes of these crises in Africa... Foday Sankoh? Whatever ideals he had as a revolutionary seeking change for his people disappeared the day he became a serious political contender in Sierra Leone... like most other African leaders... the diamond mining multinationals; and through them our governments and his own parasitic allies are on to him now to maintain the status-quo... of course for his own private profit also..... what a pity!."

The Chinook banked sharply to the right skirting a hilly outcrop. Doug looked through the dense rain forest and he was glad at what he saw. You could conceal a whole army under that dense rain forest, he thought. Then the Chinook started dropping altitude. They were barely just skirting the tree lines now and the pilot was busy maneuvering between hills and valleys. The helicopter crossed the main Freetown to Kenema highway, just after mile 91 with a strong drive into the adjoining forest and continued its tree-top hugging flight pattern. Doug's headphone came alive as the pilot put on the stand-by lights. Doug held up five fingers to the patrol to indicate five minutes to the drop-off-zone.

Soon, the helicopter banked and dropped altitude steadily close to the ground; and at a signal from Doug, the men started jumping even before touch-down. The aircraft was at its most vulnerable at this point and the first task of the Patrol was to secure the perimeter around it. The patrol had landed in a small clearing, barely enough to take the helicopter. Quickly they off-loaded their haversacks and kits as Doug jumped down bringing up the rear. As he hit the ground, the aircraft made a sharp turn and started to lift. There was so much noise and the smell of fuel and smoke in the air as the aircraft cleared the tree top and disappeared. Simultaneously, the Patrol sprinted in a zig-zag manner into the surrounding jungle and took cover under the thick under-brush and waited. They waited in their heavily camouflaged positions for one hour to observe any possible enemy interest in their landing. With no observed enemy interest, the Patrol emerged from their firing positions and assembled around Sergeant Doug. Darkness was creeping in; and in a few minutes, it was nightfall as it became pitch dark under the thick West African rain forest.

Abenaa sat in the small room that served as her bedroom. It was a bedroom without a bed in the proper sense; as a straw mattress thrown on the floor served as her bed. She sat up on the mattress and rested her back against the cold wall: A nervous shiver ran down her spine. She brought out a small hand-held mirror and looked at her fresh chocolate face. Abenaa! You are beautiful, she spoke to herself softly. Next, she swivelled the mirror down to take in her full frontally provocative breasts. Ripe and robust, she thrust them into her palms and massaged them softly. She reached for a glass of water and rolled the tepid liquid round her mouth and swallowed. She felt good as the coolness of the water spread from her throat to her chest and stomach.

Her thoughts went back to that morning and she felt, happy, well-rested and fulfilled. She had betrayed Captain Mondei, had been unfaithful but she somehow did not feel guilty about it. She had feebly asked Martin to stop; even whilst she wanted and actually enjoyed it. As she remembered the encounter, a warm glow came over her and she was all wet again. She could not really deny it now. That she made her medical nursing visit to Squadron Leader Martin Ikeke on purpose. She had noticed the routine since those difficult months at the height of Martin's medical difficulties. The section where she resided with the prisoners usually got very quiet as the aides and guards join in the morning physical drills and parades; and since the death of Mark Burden, Martin has had the very small room at the end of the corridor to himself. With Captain Denning taking time off every morning to jog around the camp, the opportunity to have the privacy of the entire wing to themselves had been there for sometime. But Abenaa, ever coquettish but never saying 'yes' had prevented Martin from making progress until that morning.

True, she put up a feeble resistance when Martin grabbed her from the rear and cupped her two ripe breasts in his hands. But when he turned her round and thrust his tongue into her mouth to hush her up, she knew her resistance was over. She knew she could have stopped him… but the thought of Mondei, close to two years without a word. Not even a post card; and all the hints, insinuations and rumours by aides about a possible mishap befalling him! No, she did not feel any sense of betrayal. She had not made love to a man in close to two years! Even whilst Mondei was around, he didn't make love to her very often. Always, he had complaints about things going wrong with the war; the 'Papay' getting over-bearing and getting it all wrong… and straying from the original mission of the revolution. Either that or he was far away in the war fronts. He would come home so tired, promptly fall asleep and got up so early to prepare for the morning 'tattoo' and parade reviews that often, there was hardly time spent together between them for her to tempt him into a deep, romantic entanglement. But Squadron Leader Martin Ikeke had done it three times in one morning. She jumped up from the bed, took another sip of water and went to the corner of the window; her favourite corner from where she observed Martin's goings and comings around the camp when she longed to see him. The next morning was even better. Martin was waiting in his room. He stood up and came over to her with arms out-stretched to cuddle her. She held him off tentatively, feebly.

"Martin… what are we doing? This is extremely dangerous… please let's stop this before it is too late."

"Should we? I feel so happy… doesn't this make you happy too?"

"I know what you mean… I feel like… like I am floating… in paradise… it must be really beautiful in heaven if this is what it feels like there" She closed her eyes as her moist lips parted to receive his. She felt his firm body against hers, stiffening, hardening as his strong biceps grabbed and tucked her into himself. His mid-section went stiff, with her groin throbbing against his hard erection pressing against her now very wet vagina region. She moaned involuntarily, unable to control her joy and excitement. She was on the edge of the window frame, leaning back in his arms, with his insistent deliberate weight bearing down on her. They fell in unison unto the straw mattress. As they fell, he pulled up her nursing uniform and entered her boldly, deliberately in swift, measured strokes. She raised her buttocks to give him full penetration and traction and a moan of satisfaction and joy escaped his lips. They were now both breathing very fast and entangled in sweat. As the enchanting body aroma of their sweat blended with the sweet smell of semen and vaginal fluid, Martin was excited unto a fresh erection and they started all over again. And again, and again.

"That was good... you are so sweet" Martin muttered wearily. Abenaa nodded groggily in response..

"You too... you are pure honey... thank you very much... thank you my love".

The SAS DeepQuest Patrol quickly adjusted to the thick West African jungle darkness. With all their faces blackened, they blended into the night. The night was hot and humid and the humidity immediately had its effect. Doug called over his two covering men, earlier deployed to cover the Patrol from about fifty meters away to a quick 'O' group meeting. In very hushed tones, since sound travelled very far at night, they agreed to commence tabbing immediately to put sufficient distance between them and the landing zone; but only after one hour of acclimatization to their new environment. The patrol had agreed to use night vision equipment to steal a huge tactical advantage over the RUF and with their night vision goggles on; they commenced tabbing on a south-easterly course. They tabbed very slowly, checking and re-checking their positions until they picked a well concealed night-stop position. Doug posted look-outs and ordered rest-stop. The position was ideal, a natural dug-out probably an old dried up stream, with its hilly banks providing a fine perimeter ring and line of sight for the look-outs. They slept, rested and exchanged look out roles throughout the night.

The next morning, Doug did a limited Recce of their surrounding and posted two heavily camouflaged look-outs on top of two adjoining tall trees about a hundred meters apart. The Patrol sent off the first radio message, properly encrypted to confirm position and progress of the DeepQuest mission so far. Night two. The Patrol commenced proper tabbing in a general north-easterly direction towards Camp 44, if the intelligence was right. With night vision equipment, they had a visual and psychological advantage. Four hours into the Patrol, it was shocked from the rear, with a deep-throated grunt followed simultaneously by an attack. Doug, leading the Patrol in front reacted instantly. "Take cover, take cover, take cover" not sure of what the nature of the attack was.

He turned, and saw a flash and a piercing shrill from Lance Corporal Andy, his signaler, who fell with a thud, with the weight of the radio equipment bearing down and smashing his head. Another deep grunt and a second charge was cut short by a dull cough from a silenced 203 rifle. It was the season of the wild boar, what the creoles of Sierra Leone call "bush pig". Wild, ferocious beasts that usually hunt at night and would attack without warning. The boar had aimed at Andy's groins; and only a last-minute instinctive turn saved Andy's privates, but the entire flesh around his right thigh bone had been ripped off during the attack. Andy was in uncontrollable pains and his cries carried far into the night, threatening to breach the mission's security. All six members of the patrol were medically trained and knew what to do. Andy ripped off the morphine ampoule from around his neck and gave some to Doug, who promptly stabbed the injection into his buttock. The effect was instantaneous as Andy floated away into a temporary comfort zone that sedated him as it eased his pains. Doug brought out field dressing and had Andy's thighs dressed.

Next, he turned his attention to the pitch-black evil looking boar. A boar with a bullet wound, and a lot of blood spilled would surely breach mission security. The dead boar and the blood would attract vultures and flies... which in turn would attract human interest... which would lead to a lot of unanswered questions: Who shot the boar? Was it shot for food? What kind of bullet was used? If shot for food, why would an army or local populace in search of food shoot and abandon a prime source of protein like the boar? Doug, for operational security had to make two quick decisions. First, he ordered a total clean up of all the blood stains and ordered a make-shift hearse to carry the boar. Slowed down by the weight of the boar and an injured Andy, the patrol made very little progress.

Then, that little element of luck that every operation needs came the patrol's way. The heavens opened up to a torrential rainfall. Under cover, Doug heaved a sigh of relief. Under the rain, the patrol prepared a make-shift grave for the boar, threw it and its makeshift hearse into it and had the grave promptly covered with earth; leaving the pouring rain to clear up any tell-tale signs. Doug ordered a resumption of their tabbing to put as much distance between the patrol and the boar's burial site. Two hours later, just before dawn, he ordered a rest stop for the day.

The rain stopped abruptly as dawn broke. As the sun broke through the rain- swept clouds, the look-out rushed down to tap Doug to wake up from his nap.

They crawled up to a vantage point and peered through their binoculars: An RUF patrol, with AK-47 slung over their shoulders was cutting its way through the thick under-brush with careless abandon. As Doug watched; he saw the leader make a sign for silence and take cover and the patrol went down in stillness. The RUF patrol leader put his fingers into his mouth to imitate the sound of a crow. He made the sound three times and emerged from cover. From what Doug thought was an anthill, a response came, as three RUF soldiers emerged from the base of the anthill to cheers from the retuning RUF patrol. The anthill unit and the returning RUF patrol, now of about a company strength as they emerged from the jungle exchanged pleasantries, backslapping and cheers; all these less than a hundred meters from the SAS "DeepQuest" Patrol. In no time, the RUF Company had a fire burning, tea brewing, distilled alcohol in cellophane sachets were passed round. After a very loud breakfast, the company cleaned up all signs of cooking, drinking and smoking; very professionally burying all signs of waste and went into a disciplined rest stop routine.

What the SAS Patrol had picked as an ideal day rest stop location had similarly been picked by the RUF Company. Six hours of tension ensued. Instead of the envisaged rest, the patrol was on the edge; with all men in firing positions and fighting knives drawn from their sheath. They watched and listened as some of the RUF soldiers came close to answer the calls of nature, carelessly thrusting out their manhood to urinate. It was by now past the mandatory daily Situation Report time for the Operations Room at the Forward Operating Base. But the Patrol dared not make a move for fear of attracting the RUF's attention. Doug and the other members of the Patrol stared down the sights of their cocked rifles at the RUF position for what seemed an eternity. Four hours later, and at the blast of a whistle, the company re-assembled and moved on in single file, with the officer commanding, a tall dark, young Lieutenant leading the rear. He took the salute of the Anthill Observation Post occupants sharply and departed.

Phew! Doug whistled to himself. He was shocked that the entire mission was close to being compromised through sheer carelessness. How could they have wandered into the RUF O.P., under the intense rain the previous night without realizing it? For answers, he gazed intently at the innocent looking anthills through his binoculars. There must be a network of underground bunkers housing the O.P. unit, with holes on the anthill itself for the lookouts. He ordered total silence and deep camouflage for the rest of the day; which was uneventful. The Patrol set off at dusk and promptly ran into difficulties. The bitten signaller, Andy had slept all day; but unknown to the patrol had become rabied. Despite the good field dressing of his injuries and anti-tetanus injections, he had been infected with a deadly strain of boar rabies and was losing blood steadily through a punctured artery. The six-man patrol was consequently slowed down to a walk. Three hours into the walk, Andy broke down in sweat and convulsion and could move no more. As the pains and infection got into his blood-stream and central nervous system, Andy lost control of all his senses and started a deep guttural grunt involuntarily. A drink of water was offered to calm him down but he threw up the water and all he had eaten in a smelling vomit.

At that point, Doug knew the Patrol had a serious problem. Andy could not proceed with the Patrol and his involuntary grunts could breach their operational security and compromise the Patrol's location. He therefore decided on an emergency evacuation to the Forward Operating Base. The two-man reconnaissance party sent to establish an appropriate medical evacuation loading strip for the Huey helicopter returned about twelve noon the next day; soaking wet and all muddied up from the rainfall; but returned with good intelligence all the same. The patrol promptly followed their trail heading in a north-westerly direction until they hit the narrow rendezvous in the dense jungle at about five in the evening. They lay in deep cover. Forty minutes later, the pilot's voice cracked through on the radio. The DeepQuest Patrol acknowledged the pilot and repeated the co-ordinates of the rendezvous. They were still in deep cover and deployed at reasonable intervals from each other around the small clearing. Not being a night flight, the night approach, using night vision equipment and infra-red signals were abandoned for a direct visual approach at the sight of an orange flare. As the whoosh of the helicopter rotor came closer, Doug ignited and threw the orange flare into the clearing. Three minutes later, with the flares billowing into the sky, the helicopter popped out of the tree-top and swiveled around the clearing, to give the two wing gunners a clear line of sight in case of trouble. The pilot repeated the call sign… and Doug answered in the affirmative and gave the all-clear. Quickly, Andy was rushed into the clearing in a make-shift stretcher, and straight into the helicopter. As Andy was strapped down by the medics, the DeepQuest patrol retreated back to their perimeter cover to offer covering fire for the departing helicopter.

The entire operation had lasted just under four minutes. But it was enough time. An RUF patrol, on a reconnaissance mission nearby had been attracted to the scene by the noise of the helicopter. As they rushed into the clearing, they saw the helicopter circling overhead and engaged it with ineffective rifle fire.

The two wing gunners pelted the RUF with intense machine gun fire. A rocket blast from the Huey sent the entire RUF patrol and the clearing into pandemonium. The SAS maintained strict silence under cover throughout to avoid being compromised. Whilst the RUF was licking its wounds from the attack; and with darkness creeping in, the DeepQuest patrol sneaked out of the scene in pairs, with instruction to link up at their agreed rendezvous.

After four days of Patrol and one casualty due to a boar attack; the DeepQuest party came across the first deep – wooded military encampment. Concealed in deep cover and adjoining hills, the patrol watched as life returned to the camp that morning. There were over fifty bamboo and raffia palm living apartments in the deep of the forest, all concealed from the air. There were additional tents and a browned zinc cover for what looked like an open kitchen. One of the bamboo buildings had an open clearing in front. The building had a black cable running from it into an adjoining tree trunk; and all the way to the top of the tree, where an antenna was barely visible. As Doug peered through his binoculars, windows and doors were thrown up and soldiers in fatigue lined up on the clearing in front of what obviously looked like the Command Post. As the soldiers filed out for the morning parade, Doug estimated the camp to be of battalion strength. The DeepQuest Patrol watched proceedings at the Camp for a whole day without any sign of Captain Denning: But at least, the Camp provided a bearing. From the sketches provided by the Intelligence Group, Doug suspected that the camp could be the RUF so called Camp Twenty-Two; which should place Camp Forty-Four in a north-easterly direction from their position. At the daily Situation Report that evening, he provided the details of the camp and its co-ordinates. After an 'O' group meeting, the patrol set off in the general direction of Camp Forty-Four.

Two nights of continuous tabbing later and the Patrol hit the foot of the Sula Mountain. Doug consulted the Patrol and insisted that inch-by-inch they must climb to the top of the mountain to circumvent the heavy fortifications and military presence on the flat land approach. The top of the Sula Mountain gave only a slight hint of military presence on the base of the mountain. But by the time the patrol inched their way down below tree-level, it was an awesome sight that they beheld. There were rows and rows of bamboo and thatched roofed buildings running against the foot of the mountain. Another set of bamboo and raffia buildings were etched against tree-trunks and ran for over three hundred metres. For over three hours that morning, the entire DeepQuest Patrol was glued to binoculars taking in the awesome sight. There were black cables running into wireless antennas mounted on various tree-tops from the main building in the camp etched into the Southern foot of the mountain. Obviously the Command Post, two flags fluttered on top of the building. Tents were strewn everywhere. Through some unknown bush paths, bicycles, motor cycles and four deeply camouflaged Land Rovers were parked in front of the Command Post, off-loading supplies mostly ammunition, medicines and food. The supplies were loaded into what looked like an underground ammunition storage.

DeepQuest was now deployed lower downhill to the north-west and was now looking directly into the camp, taking in all the breath-taking actions. As Doug peered through the binoculars, he thought about what damage six professional soldiers could inflict on the camp. Approach the camp undetected, detonate the underground ammunition dump, plant timed devices in assorted areas, retreat to the hills and detonate... Movements down in the camp brought him back from his thoughts. Well-kitted soldiers were falling- in, parade fashion. Properly kitted with ammunition pouches, belts, webbings, bayonets, drinking water bottles. At different ends of the camp, there were four Oerlikon anti-aircraft guns mounted on mobile emplacements, wheel-mounted Browning 30 machine guns, and Russian-made Goryunova SG43 machine guns. As he looked, Doug saw an army stocked by the world's biggest black market of military hardware. There were Kalashnikovs AK47s, Uzis, Stens, Sterling's, M1s, M2s and Belgian Fabriquen National FN rifles. There were even vintage Mark-2s and Remington shotguns. Doug wondered how the army coped with the different array of weaponry and the logistics nightmare to manage the ammunition requirements..

At six in the morning, the garrison was awakened by the reveille bugle. More men poured into the parade ground and lined up for inspection. As the assembled men noticed the arrival of an officer on the higher ground, they all came to attention, prepared for inspection. The bugler played the RUF and the Sierra Leone National Anthems. There was an address and three hearty cheers and the heavily-kitted battalion departed in single file and disappeared into the far – end of the camp, probably headed for battle. At about seven that morning, Doug saw what he was looking for. The sight of a lone white man in shorts and singlet jogging vigorously down the southern end of the camp. Doug tapped the other members of the Patrol to take a look through their binoculars. For all of one hour, they watched the Captain looking well conditioned, tough sinewy muscles stride through the plantation in graceful motion. Two hours later, they watched the captain return into a set of housing built into the foot of the Southern end of the camp. He re-emerged almost immediately with a bath towel slung over his neck. They watched him as he walked all the way to the eastern end of the camp, where he descended downhill behind foliage. When he returned into view, he was walking briskly, bare-chested and looking fresh. Throughout the day, the Patrol watched his every movement in uniform with a group of cadets, in uniform going into the Command Post, in the open grounds with the cadets and playing volleyball with Martin and Abenaa in the evening. After the game of volleyball, he moved over to the south end foliage, again with his towel slung across his shoulders: That night, Doug provided the latest update in his Situation Report to the Forward Operation Base. "Denny boy sighted. Preparing to make contact" was the terse and precise message that sent the planning echelon all the way through the FOB to the Ministry of Defence in London brimming with excitement.

To get a proper view of the layout and what Captain Denning does twice a day at the south – east end of the camp behind the foliage, the Patrol worked their way inch-by-inch delicately on the mountain edge to the south east of the camp. It was tough going in pitch darkness, using night vision goggles. They climbed all through the night, getting a vantage position just before dawn. With a concealed location secured, they awaited the morning reveille bugle. It came promptly at six in the morning. But what they had gained by tactical advantage on the southeast by establishing the presence of a stream and dug-out toilets also robbed them of a full view into the camp to watch the morning parade and all other movements in the camp. At about half-past eight that morning, Captain Denning walked briskly to a slight incline, adjoining the stream and entered an area fenced off with raffia palms. From the set up, Doug suspected, it was a pit latrine. The Captain spent about ten minutes inside, re-emerged, stretched himself and went into the stream for a slow and gentle bath. After that, he took a few breast-strokes as he swam leisurely back and forth. He came out, cleaned himself up with a towel and whistled his way back to his quarters. The Patrol studied the entire layout throughout the day on how best to make contact with Captain Denning.

That night, with his face totally blackened, Doug crept down the over looking hill to take position inside the camp. He skirted perimeter defences and the roving sentries and went straight into the latrine area. With his night vision goggles, he checked for any possible hiding place. An over-hanging tree branch dropping into the latrine area looked attractive; but he dismissed the position for being too exposed and vulnerable. To hang around the latrine area? What if some other user, probably RUF came to use the latrine? Finally, he decided on climbing inside the latrine itself. Fortunately it was not a deep and proper African pit latrine but really a converted pit with strong logs, arranged across on top with undulating shoulders large enough to hold the frame of Doug by the side away from the reception point for the human stools proper. With the stench of the faeces and flies for company, Doug lay in wait, looking out for the only Caucasian buttock in Camp Forty Four.

There were three early users including a female user of the facility that morning. By half past eight, Captain Denning whistling and humming Frank Sinatra's "My way" came into the clearing, undressed and squatted.

"Captain Denning! Please, don't bother to look down. This is the SAS... We have come to take you home!"

"But I am having fun here... I don't want to leave... this is home to me now!"

"Please Captain... it is difficult as it is for us already as you can see from my position... please don't make things even more difficult for us.. please... we must take you with us..."

"Must? You are not in a position to give me orders here... you are not exactly in a position to even give orders... knowing that I can compromise your mission even right now..."

"No, you won't, you are an officer and gentleman of the British army..."

"You will not teach me patriotism... Let me think about it... and I will leave a message here... under this log of wood (tapping the log) later this evening. Goodbye..."

Captain Denning returned to the latrine later in the evening after his exercises. He had written a bold "No" on a piece of paper and was adjusting the piece of log to put the piece of paper under when Doug called out.

"Captain... are you back? What's the answer?"

"Jesus! You mean you are still here... been here the whole day? What gives you the kick to do these things... Money? Fame? Or just the adrenaline? Definitely not patriotism... not when the politicians have messed up our image everywhere!"

"Captain... I am just a soldier doing my job... obeying orders from superior officers like you!"

"Okay... you win... see here (revealing the 'No' piece of paper) I had scribbled a 'no' for you to take back to them, but for your sake... just for your sake... I will come with you..."

"Thank you Sir, tomorrow 18.30 hours... so that we can use the darkness after that... Thank you... see you tomorrow"

For Abenaa, the nights these days and the long wait for dawn had become agonizing. She lived in expectant turmoil, some internal longing and revolt that would gnaw her entrails all through the night until dawn brought her lover again. The very sight of the tall, well-built Martin stirred her; his spiritely figure in uniform caused internal agitation and palpitations. Just the mention of his name in casual discussion excited her innermost emotions. All through her sleepless nights, she constructed love poems in her head and recited them over and over until she could grab some sleep. The way they saw each other now and then under the garb of official duties and the quickly stolen romances at dawn had so much rigid constraints and high risk of exposure... the possibility of being caught and the possibility of scandal pumped up her blood pressure and libido instead of discouraging her. Greeting him officially on the corridors and walkways was sheer punishment; as she had to disguise the rhythmic palpitation in her heart and the hunger for his touch that her body desired. On some of the days, they would meet by "sheer accident" at the camp's clinic for the now almost daily aspirin for his headaches. Her gentle massaging of his forehead to relieve the headaches in the midst of strong smells of antiseptics, morphines and anti-biotics had a special sensual meaning. Afterwards, they would accidentally hold hands and steal warmth from each other; without consummating their burning hunger for each other. They would play volleyball with Brett and rush straight together to the stream for a cool swim, maintaining officiousness and agonizing detachment. If the sentries, aides and batmen suspected anything, they never gave an inkling as the two lovers walked back together after their daily games.

"Oh Abenaa; you are so sweet, so natural, so unpretentious... My entire life has been changed by you." Martin told her that morning. She was supremely happy that morning. She gave a warm, inviting smile and cut off the beginning of another romantic speech from Martin with a deep all-embracing kiss – lips, tongue, teeth saliva and all. They were two siamese twins joined in their mouths at that instance. They broke apart – only momentarily. They were in each other's arms again and Abenaa was doing the talking this time.

"Martin... you know I feel at ease... when we do this... I don't feel like... how do I put it... like a cheat... like an unfaithful wife, if you know what I mean"

"Oh, Abenaa... you are not... why would you even think of such things now... when you are with me... Here we are in love... but cannot proclaim it... what burden to bear! What punishment! We are surfing through life... yes some heavenly kisses... but yet unfulfilled,because we have to hide and seek each other..what a life!!!"

"It's more than that" she cut him short "sweet, intimate love making, caring for each other... We fit together... complement each other... You are my everything... you see things differently with your sharp intellect... you are a modern, cosmopolitan, international citizen of the world... I am more of a natural village brought- up girl... my values are still very native and traditional..."

"But that's what makes you so different... that is why you are so committed to the things you do... the truth Abenaa is that we belong together... we can do more together... but look how artificial our life here is... look at us stealing kisses... Thank God... we can resolve this absurd situation now!"

She was jolted, taken aback, now filled with wild desire and fear at the same time... she grabbed Martin much more tightly, pushing her breast against his broad chest... she looked straight into his eyes and asked sharply

"What exactly do you mean?"

"A.B... I am a serious lover and I am man enough to admit I cannot live without you... that I will not step out of this camp without you... what freedom can be out there if you are not part of it?"

Her face lit up in childish excitement briefly before it was overtaken by a brooding feeling. She looked different now... sad and sullen; a grave sense of melancholy suddenly overtook her. She leaned against him and said quietly...

"But I am married... how can you possibly take me away from my husband?"

He stared back at her, self-assured and very confident.

"You mean, you were married... you are not married now... you have not been married for close to two years now... and you know it..."

"But he would come back someday… I know he would…"

"Ab… no! He won't come back…. Listen to me (seizing her gently and clasping her face to his eyes) "Look at my lips… look at my eyes… believe me when I say he would not be coming back… he is dead… was killed"

She stepped back suddenly, staring at him. She snatched a pillow, threw it at him and missed… she grabbed another pillow and buried her face in it, weeping. Her face was now drawn and melancholic as she sobbed uncontrollably into the pillow.

He was now pleading. He had reverted to a wise avuncular role… the father figure rationally pleading for her to see reason. He knew this was going to be a difficult phase. The moment he discussed with Captain Brett Denning and he unfolded the escape plot, they were both unanimous in their resolve not to leave Camp 44 without Abenaa. He heard his voice going deeply authoritative, but emotional

"You, loving, innocent baby…" he said as he pulled her to himself closely "can't you see the hurt in my eyes? You are hurting me so badly… and you don't know it… I love you…" His move had broken the tension and he saw that emotional longing for his hugging coming back into her eyes.

"You were married to him in good faith… he was an idealist… he believed in the cause and the revolution that followed… but his leaders let him down… so they killed him… I thought you should know… But I am here for you… I will take you out of here with me tonight… don't worry…"

"Who killed him?"

"Who else… the old man, the 'Papay'… killed him and the two others for challenging his authority… they did not go to Libya… everybody else knew… except you…"

"So you have been exploiting my situation?"

"A-B… Me? Prey on you? I know you don't believe that yourself. I love you… I will care for you… I will cherish you all the days of my life. 'A.B.' you deserve a better life than you are getting. You will be my wife… can't you see we love each other?"

From the edge of his eyes, he saw Abenaa's gentle nod of acceptance and he knew he had conquered her emotions.

They held on to each other for a long time in silence. "Say something" Abenaa said

"No. Let's listen to the voice of silence as I listen to your heart beating... so positive, so romantic... can't you hear it?"

In the silence that followed, entwined in romantic thoughts, staring at each other's confident eager eyes... slowly tears rolled down their eyes, blurring their vision as he thrust his tongue into her mouth. Inseparably entwined, and in blissful ecstasy, they fell asleep in each other's arms.

They played volleyball that evening; and it was not unusual for them to head towards the stream on the southern tip of the camp for a swim after games. But this evening, Abenaa had clothes in a duffel bag for washing. True, she washed some inconsequential shirts and shorts and returned to the cloth line to hang them out in the sun. Conveniently, she left behind three khaki trousers and skirt and three jungle boots. Captain Denning had a long swim and even a longer time in the latrine responding to his diarrhea which mysteriously hit all three – Abenaa, Martin and Brett that morning. For that reason, all three had frequented the latrine all day, with sympathetic glances from the student cadets. They were still taking their turns at the pit latrine when darkness enveloped the camp. That was when they changed to their boots, khaki trousers and shirts. It was about the same time that Doug emerged from the undergrowth, gave them night vision goggles and led them, crawling through dark foliage, between the sentries and prowling guards into the adjoining hills. It took thirty minutes of hard climbing and crawling for them to rendezvous with the DeepQuest patrol.

Once out of ear – shot and back with the patrol, Doug raised the issue of the extra persons. That his mission and clear instruction was to bring home Captain Denning. So who were these other passengers? Brett explained who they were and how they must all be evacuated as a group.

"Well, Sir... those are not my orders... they can't come with us... especially the woman, she is going to slow us down and jeopardize the success of the mission"

"Sergeant! You have your orders… but you have done your bit… I take charge now as your superior officer… they are both coming with us"

"Sir" Doug snapped, saluting sharply "You cannot throw rank at me… I don't care what rank you wear on those pampered shoulders of yours… I am in charge of this patrol and you damn well know that only the Mission Commander at the Forward Operating Base can change my orders…"

"Then call him… damn you… what insolence!! Or we might as well walk back to the camp and you risk the failure of your mission" Brett snapped.

"You do not understand Sir! You do not have a choice in the matter… any sign of resistance on your part… and these men have clear orders to immobilize you and take you back home… whether you like it or not… so don't push your luck… and don't push us Sir!…….. Gary… see whether you can raise FOB and re-confirm the extraction rendezvous… see also whether you can get an okay for the two passengers… Mason, Jack… set the explosives… time the explosions for six, seven and eight tomorrow morning for diversion…"

Very business-like, Doug was now the complete soldier, the thoroughbred SAS man with so many mission accomplishments in different theatres of conflicts around the world. No friendship, no emotions, he stormed past Captain Denning as if he didn't exist as the FOB came through. The Okay came through the airwaves…

"Denny boy plus two passengers" and with that, the group started the tortuous circuitous climb back to the North-end of Camp Forty-Four. It took all of eight hours to circum-navigate and climb down the mountain down to the Wara Wara forest and the adjoining flat lands. After a one hour rest stop, they continued the tabbing at a fast pace, arriving at the Rendezvous at dawn.

The first sign of trouble at Camp Forty-Four was after the morning reveille, when unusually Captain Denning did not do his jogging. A worried Doctor Frazier, who was aware of his complaints of diarrhea the previous day went over to the prisoners' quarters to check on him; and found the room empty. He knocked and went into Martin's room and found it similarly empty. He quickly drew the attention of the Brigade Major and the Chief of Intelligence to the development, since the "Papay" and the other senior officers were away to the Zimmi front. The camp was thrown into a frenzy as search units were quickly mobilized.

That was when the first set of explosions went off at the southern end of the camp. A mad rush ensued as more and more soldiers were deployed in the direction of the explosions. With more explosions an hour later in the same general south-westerly direction, the RUF soldiers were convinced that the escaped prisoners had headed south into the Tonkolili forest, where the search was then concentrated.

The Puma came in at tree-top and initially over-shot the small clearing. Then Doug hauled the locator flares into the clearing to provide the Puma pilot a better visual approach and the helicopter made a sharp right bank and came in very fast. The doors were swung open in that instant, but the aircraft stayed aloft until it was joined by two Apache attack helicopters on both wings serving as escorts. The Apaches peeled off to opposite ends of the clearing halted in mid-air, with their guns and rockets trained on possible enemy threats. Then the Puma came down quickly. Doug pushed the prisoners forward while the rest of the patrol provided perimeter cover. With everyone on board, the three helicopters took off in formation with the Apaches providing wing cover right and left. Just over one hour later, they were on the deck of the aircraft carrier; and in a most dramatic manner, that marked the end of over two years of captivity for Brett and Martin.

The car lumbered slowly along the Accra-Swedru road. An Old Opel Kadett, it was the only one available out of Accra after they had been stranded in the capital city for over four days... At the control of the wheels was Kwame, the dark, bulky, bearded and very talkative driver. Plodding slowly but surely ahead, Kwame gave a running commentary as they swung round the Swedru inter-change.

"The road to the right goes to Winneba... That's where we have our sports university... all our footballers train there before any major competition... Massa... you know Abedi Pele? Good striker... he is in the Black Stars camp now in Winneba preparing for the African Nations Cup" Kwame announced to the occupants of the car.

The side-streets were a mixed collection of fruits and 'Kenke' sellers. Farmers, fresh from the day's farm harvest swung by as they rubbed shoulders with younger folks who peered into the Opel Kadett and ogled the pretty looking European lady at the back seat of the car. They drove all through the evening, with a brief stop-over at Saltpond for nature's call. Just before midnight, they pulled into Sanaa Lodge in Cape Coast. Stepping down from the car, Brett took in the breath- taking water-front view, complete with the coconut grove and fishing boats of Cape Coast as he crossed into the reception hall of the hotel. There was a very polite lady at the reception desk; who also politely told Brett, there was no room available; that the town was in a festive mood with the Afyashe festival. After so many disappointments, they finally settled in at the Oyster Bay hotel very early that morning. The Oyster Bay was a nice hotel. With unique round hut designs petched on the Atlantic beach, the roaring waves were musical to the tired frames of the travellers.

The flight into Accra on British Airways was smooth, uneventful. Sue slept all through the day-time flight. But their problems started upon arrival. They had flown into a country where a nation-wide labour strike over sundry matters - price of petrol, cocoa, bread, and wages, inflation etc- had ground the country to a halt. Kwame, the driver had explained it all as "Kumi Preku" that the people were prepared for instant death via confrontation with the authorities, instead of the instalmental death that had become their lot under the harsh policies of the government.

The nation-wide strike caught and had the Dennings stranded at the airport; and crucially also meant that Martin and Abenaa could not come through by road from Nigeria through the Aflao border. So, after months and months of pain-staking planning for the re-union of the two former RUF prisoners on a frantic mission to save Sue Denning; the Dennings had finally made it to Cape Coast in Ghana. That morning, Brett and Sue slept in each other's arms, with doors and windows wide open to receive the fresh winds of the Atlantic Ocean. Brett slept soundly and drifted away to Hereford......

Captain Denning was flown from the Forward Operating Base aircraft carrier into the hands of a provost unit of the Parachute Regiment and taken under military escort and in handcuffs to a military base in Chelsea. For the next two weeks, he went through a battery of tests - X-Rays, blood and urine tests, post-traumatic stress tests, psycho-analysis test, HIV test. The tests revealed a mild cough and cerebral malaria for which treatment was commenced immediately. Critically, the medical people ran repeated HIV and Neurosis tests and found Brett was negative and he was therefore returned to the Provost Command, who promptly put him in solitary confinement for the next two weeks.

Exactly two weeks after his return, the grilling started. The Parachute Regiment went through every detail of Brett's stay in Sierra Leone. What manner of military training did he give to the RUF cadets? Why did he refuse escape and evacuation initially? Where and when did he pick up the alleged HIV infection? The Military Intelligence and Special Investigation Panel squeezed him for over one week on every piece of knowledge of any intelligence value he had of the RUF. Then they played transcripts of his interviews with the Africa Service of the BBC.....

"An Officer and gentlemen of the Parachute Regiment... Captain that rank that you wear puts a certain responsibility on your shoulders... looking back now... are you proud of your performance during the BBC interview?" The question came from Brigadier Anthony Russel; Head of the Special Investigation Panel (SIP) of the Court Martial proceedings.

"What aspect of the interview would you be referring to Sir?"

"Let me remind you, Captain and... I quote... : Britain has no business getting involved and fueling the crisis in the first place... what was I doing in Sierra Leone? I was training and arming one side to the conflict in Sierra Leone on behalf of the British Government... why don't we use our colonial influence and authority to broker peace instead of instigating wars? Unquote... Was that you speaking... Captain? and do you still maintain that position?"

"Yes Sir!"

"What about this Captain... Quote:... If you take the technical definition of the term mercenary... yes I was a mercenary... I was paid, do I say my total emoluments were far, far higher than my equivalent in the Sierra Leone army... and I was a foreign combatant in a general sense... since I contributed to the Sierra Leonean war effort... unquote.... Captain, were you deployed to Sierra Leone as a mercenary?" "

Sir! I said "technically"... yes technically I was a mercenary!!"

"So you were not under any form of duress when you granted that interview?"

"Not at all Sir!" There was absolute silence around the room. More out of anger and frustration, Brigadier Russel decided to needle and humiliate Brett by probing into his health problems.

"Captain... Where did you pick up the clap? The HIV clap that reduced you to servitude with the RUF... was it while frolicking as a mercenary in Freetown?" Captain Denning was calm; and proceeded without emotions.

"I am sure Sir that you know that no one in this room is competent to discuss my medical records. The state of my health is a very private and personal matter. Only the Regimental Medical Officer can discuss my health status with me because he is on a strict professional oath, but even he cannot force me to divulge my personal health matters. As for you ,not even the rank that you are trying to pull on me can force me to share my very personal health history with you... Sir!"

The SIP concluded its sitting on that note. Two weeks later, Captain Brett Denning was dishonourably discharged from the Parachute Regiment.

Squadron Leader Martin Ikeke was flown into the Lungi International Airport to a very hushed reception. Listed missing and presumed dead for over a period of two years, he was retired along with two hundred officers just three months earlier. The retirement signal had requested him to report to the Armed Forces Resettlement Center in Oshodi, Lagos for a Pre-retirement Course before eventual disengagement. With help from Rugiatu, his Sierra Leonean friend who worked with the Sierra Leone Airport Authority, Abenaa was given a place to stay near the airport. Alhaji Bashiru, another friend at the Nigerian High Commission organized a quick civil marriage at the Freetown Registry and provided Abenaa a Nigerian passport.

One week after, Martin and Abenaa arrived Lagos on a rainy morning. Met by a select group of family members, he chose to settle in Lagos to reorganize his life in Aguda Surulere, Lagos with his childhood friend, who was a senior correspondent with the Guardian newspaper. It was a period of massive deregulation of the airline industry; and with new airlines everywhere, it was quite easy for Martin to fit into a commercial flying role. It was whilst on a flight simulator training on the BAC 1-11 in England that he re-established contacts with Brett. That was when the decision to rendezvous in Accra for the search for the cure for Brett's wife was initiated.

The Ikekes boarded the car at Mile 2; and the driver had driven all the way through Badagry, through Cotonou and Lome. The drive was leisurely and very enjoyable until they got to Aflao, the border town between Ghana and Togo. There, he was to find out that an on-going nation-wide strike had thrown the gateway into Ghana firmly shut. The Aflao border post attracted a mixed collection of people that evening. Ewe speaking people on both sides of the border traversed to and fro at will with farm produce and wares for sale; feeling oblivious or disrespectful of the artificial borders imposed by the colonial heritage of the two countries. Over a three mile long convoy of stranded trailers, buses ferrying passengers,kolanuts, cement and food items were on both side of the border. Black-clad immigration officials, khaki-green wearing and gun-totting soldiers and brown-clad customs officials mingled freely with a motley crowd of passengers, traders, hustlers and garishly dressed border town prostitutes parading their wares to anyone who cared to let loose his passion.

Unable to cross the Aflao border, Martin and Abenaa spent the night in the car. They were to spend two more nights before the strike was called off and they were stamped into Ghana.

The eventual re-union of the two RUF Prisoner of War camp friends was ecstatic. On the hilly outcrop of the Atlantic Ocean where the Oyster Bay hotel was located, the two friends shared long nostalgic moments. Eventually, they came to the realization that their wives had to be integrated in what they saw as a mission. Sue appeared with a stunning tropical, multi-coloured shirt and a tight short. She exuded star quality as she perched herself delicately on Brett's laps. Abenna had grown. More womanly. A much more sophisticated carriage and a radiant black beauty. She looked stunning in her tight-fitting jean, short and Marines T-shirt; which accentuated her provocative cleavage.

"Sue... please meet Abenaa... the naturally gifted physician we have talked so much about. Abenaa... my wife Sue"

Brett continued with the introductions and moved straight into formal mission discussion.

"Let me state clearly" Brett continued "that on behalf of my wife and myself that I am extremely grateful to Abenaa for being so kind to us. Martin has explained your conditions to me – that this must not be for any commercial considerations; but purely for the sake of my wife Sue. I am grateful. Even way back in Camp 44 as prisoners, I was fully aware of the intense pressure from all the medical people around you to commercialize this your unique cure for HIV but you resisted all the temptations thrown at you. You surprise and disarm me with your humility, simplicity and commitment to your traditional values."

Brett broke off and embraced Abenaa emotionally, eased off and planted a warm peck on her cheek. "We have some distance to travel" Martin Ikeke broke in. "I have been doing a lot of preparatory reading as you can see" as he spread a political map of Ghana across the table. "We are here" as he tabbed his fingers on Cape Coast. We will have to travel North-Westerly into the Ashanti Region; where 'Ab' tells me she last saw the therapeutic reed. She says the reed grows on the banks of fast-flowing fresh-water streams... and she last saw it on the banks of the Konongo River on a trip with her father".

The next morning, the two families set off towards Konongo village via the Cape-Coast – Obuasi road. The picturesque, well-manicured, undulating road virtually hewed out of rocky hills provided a panoramic view. Two hours into the drive, they entered Ashanti region and the bull-dozers, frenzied movement of miners and security personnel welcomed them to Obuasi's famed Ashanti Gold Fields. Behind them was the serene coconut-lined shorelines of Cape Coast, capital of the Central Region of Ghana. It was a comfortable drive all through and the two families discussed with nostalgia their experiences in and the beauty of Cape Coast. Their emotionally draining visit to the Cape Coast and Elmina castles, where the story of the Trans-Atlantic slave trade was vividly retold; how the slaves were massed and squeezed through the narrow "point of no return" unto ships for the America's and Europe; and how for every one slave that made it to the so-called "New World" an estimated twenty-five died in transit.

They were among over two hundred visitors who were at the Cape-Coast and Elmina Castles on the day of their visit.

It was the "Fetu Afahye" festival period and thousands of Ghanaians had poured into the town for the carnival; and the Cape Coast Castle, now a World Heritage Site was a centre of attraction. Originally discovered by the Portuguese, who made it a stop-over point on their way to the discovery of the Americas, it was converted to a castle by the Dutch in 1637. The castle was expanded by the Swedes in 1652 and captured by the British in 1664. Gold Coast, as Ghana was earlier called was administered by the British from the Cape Coast Castle until the seat of government was moved to Accra in 1877.

In line with their cover for the mission- tourism – they had immersed themselves fully into the "Fetu Afahye" carnival. They had watched the colourful Procession of Chiefs, all the dancing and drumming and the Ritual Slaughter of cows for the seventy-seven gods of Oguaa, the traditional name of Cape Coast. They watched the "Bakatue" ceremony, the annual cutting through of sand bars to open up the Fosu lagoon to the sea, to bring more fish into the lagoon; and the symbolic casting of the royal net by the "Omahene" to declare fishing in the lagoon officially open. The Dennings and Ikekes had lunch at a busy up class restaurant, The Solace that day after the "Bakatue" ceremony and set for Cape Coast Castle. There, a tour guide took them through the history of the Castle. The wars of ownership of the Castle between the Portuguese, the Danes; the Swedes and the British. How Christopher Columbus spent time at the Castle before setting sail for the Americas – the new world.

Then, the tour guide came to the chilly narration of the slave trade, the expeditions to capture slaves in the West African hinterland and how Cape Coast Castle was like a huge garrison and warehouse to hold thousands of slaves captured in the Gold coast and the neighbouring Ashanti, Yoruba, Benin, Igbo, Mandingo, Mende, Dahomey, Ewe and Temne Kingdoms.

As the narrator and guide took them through the back stairways and secret doors that led to secret bedrooms where young, pretty native slaves were taken for regular sexual assaults, rapes and sodomy, the air grew thicker and the silence became deafening. It became so surreal as Sue and Abenaa heard the trailing voice of the guide as if from a long distance "… a lot of these young female slaves were defiled repeatedly by officers and men of the garrison… Many were made pregnant and could therefore not stand the strain of the long trans-Atlantic journey. They died in the course of the voyages and were cast off mid-sea. Some had pronounced pregnancies before the arduous voyages and were therefore set free by the garrison commanders… to go back into the city of Cape Coast to give birth to the bastard white products of their mindless rape… that's why there are so many fair skinned people amongst the people of Cape Coast and environs of today!….. This is the last point"… the guide said with dramatic melancholy….

"You can see it is appropriately marked The Point of No Return… Here the concrete passage into the jetty and the ships had been deliberately built narrowly to eliminate stampede and resistance. The slaves were forced into a narrow single – file and pushed through this narrow point unto ready ships that took them into slavery..away from their homelands and their people forever...... And to an uncertain future in the strange lands on the other side of the Atlantic Ocean !!!" It was too much for the two wives at this point. Sue who had been clutching firmly to the shoulders of Abenaa all the while for support suddenly noticed that the shoulders were sagging; about the same time that she herself lost consciousness. There was pandemonium as Sue and Abenaa laid prostrate on the cold floor, unconscious.In the ensuing panic, somebody appeared with a large jar of water... Martin, who had a plastic jar of water that he was sipping from during the guided tour emptied the entire content on the heads of the two wives.

More water. More panic. Finally, the two wives came to; and were led delicately out of the castle into the refreshing relief of the sea breeze under the coconut trees.

As they drove into the Obuasi area of Ashanti, another image of Ghana flooded through the mind of Brett. An image of giant Western multi-nationals burrowing into the African landmass to search for gold.

A pervasive sense of guilt had gripped the Dennings since the visit to the Cape Coast Castle. Slave trade. The Trans-Atlantic slave trade. One survivor for every twenty-five shipped across the Atlantic. Taking the very virile, productive age bracket away from the development requirements back home in Africa. Into an uncertain future; that manpower gap could cripple any society. Now, the same people, who put Africans on those Trans-Atlantic slave ships and into slavery were once again putting them to burrow the earth in search of gold for peanuts!

"I am so sorry, Martin" Brett intoned involuntarily. Martin Ikeke, roused from his own thoughts expressed surprise.

"For what?" he asked.

"For everything. Let's say for the slavery and the slave trade... and generally for the sins of my forefathers"

"Forget it. This is a new generation. A new world and we must respect our common humanity and stand up for each other"

"Thanks"

That afternoon after a long drive through Kumasi, Sunyani and Berekum, they arrived at New Fetenta!.

New Fetenta was a sprawling new town, with modern brick buildings, staff quarters, staff club and staff schools. What about the adjoining village of Nsesereso?.,they asked.

"Nsesereso? That. It disappeared long ago along with the old Fetenta, baabarananu, Banu, Twinkuram, Dorma-Akwani, Antwinio and so many villages" was the very curt reply the two families received from their enquiries.

"What about the people?"

"Oh they were relocated, some to Sunyani and Kumasi,but mostly absorbed into new homes built by the mining company and the Konongo Timber and Plywood Company.

The Chief Security Officer of the Konongo Gold Field Corporation was of little help. He made available a list of allottees of company-provided flats from the ruins of the old Nsesereso.What about Nana Kwabena Donkor, the traditional head of Nsesereso?The Chief Security Officer suddenly turned sullen and uncooperative. He disclosed very angrily that he would rather not discuss the trouble maker; that the traditional ruler, Nana Donkor vehemently resisted the growth and development of the area; and died whilst trying to stop the bulldozers from commencement of work on the new plant over fourteen years ago.

Nsesereso and Konongo were all gone. The fast flowing Konongo stream, the adjoining Great Forest and the therapeutic reed that used to abound on its mangrove banks had all disappeared with the entry of miners and timber merchants into the area. In their place were now new mining office blocks, and large production facilities operated by the mining company. All along the banks of the now polluted Konongo river, gold processing units of the Konongo Gold Fields Corporation, heavy articulated trucks running non-stop with run of mine ore to be emptied into Gyratory Crushers; stockpiles of coarse ore, ball mills, large scavenger trains, cleaner scavengers and extrusion plants. On the exact spot, where young maidens were initiated by the river in the past, the Corporation now had a large Gravity Concentration plant, a flotation plant that fed Regrinding, Roasting, Bio-Oxidation, Pressurization and Retorting Mills for production of the final gold concentrate.

There was absolute gloom in the car as they drove back to Kumasi that night. Abenaa sobbed throughout. The loss of a father she had often willed out of her mind. The loss of a whole God-given treasure of therapeutic trees, plants and reeds, to the search for gold.

Gold! The precious metal had often occurred naturally along the streams of Nsesereso for as long as Abenaa could remember whilst growing up as a child. Every family had a gold trunk box. In school, she had been taught how Otunfor Osei Tutu had used myth, religion and spirituality to develop the Ashanti nation with the mystical powers of gold. How the legendary Okomfo Anokye, friend and spiritual adviser to Otumfo Osei Tutu had caused the heaven to send down the Golden Stool which remained the symbol of Ashanti unity till date. Gold had always been a source of joy and wealth. A pleasure to own and possess. Gold! The precious metal that gave Gold Coast its original British name; a great medium of jewelry that had adorned the necks, arms and legs of Ghanaians for ages. This visually stunning metal that conveyed mystique as a religious object, as a charm and amulet!! For this same legendary and mythical metal to be at the same time the source of her father's death, cause the disappearance of entire communities and their supporting eco-system; and now for gold to be responsible for the loss of a unique ecology that could have saved Sue Denning and mankind!!

Abenaa sobbed herself to sleep in the firm, soothing arms of Martin as they drove back through Kumasi;and all the way to Accra that night. Not a word was uttered in the car throughout the trip; but the sense of despair was pervasive.

The two couples landed at what was left of Camp 44 very early that morning. Following a combined Government and ECOMOG offensive, the strategic triangle of Makeni, Bo/Kenema and Masiaka were back in government control; and a pillaged Camp 44 lay in ruins. Gone were the living quarters, the military academy and the Papay's strategic headquarters. At the desolate corner where it had always been was the wooden shack which served as the inter-denominational church. The two wives joined Brett and Martin as they walked through the ruins in nostalgia. A burnt helmet, empty ammunition casings, burnt-out vehicles and soot lay scattered everywhere. At the end of the Camp, the secluded stream retained its natural serenity despite being a witness to the ravages of war. Spontaneously, Abenaa pulled off her clothes and plunged into the cool comfort of the stream. Quickly, everybody else undressed and plunged into the stream as the helicopter lifted off; back to Freetown.

Three days earlier, they had landed at the Lungi International Airport and to their surprise; there was now a new faster hovercraft service across the sea to Freetown. There was also a Huey helicopter shuttle service between the airport and Freetown. The two couples opted to fly across; and what a surprise!!. The back-slapping, hugging and clenched fists said more about the intimacy between Brett and the two-man crew of the helicopter. That evening at the Cotton Tree, the helicopter crew, a Russian and a South – African, former drinking pals of Brett provided updates on the current war situation. They said they had quit fighting to concentrate on the Lungi – Freetown commercial shuttle, which was much more lucrative at a hundred dollars per passenger.

Amid all the drinking and dancing, Denning hatched an outline plan in very hushed tones. Fly the two couples to Camp 44, drop them off in the morning and come back to evacuate them the next morning. A simple plan; with only one snag: Commercial flights were not allowed beyond the Masiaka/Lunsar corridor! But for Denning and an additional thousand dollars they would do anything. That was three days ago.

But back to the present at Camp 44,….. suddenly, it started raining. Heavy, tropically ferocious rain accompanied by strong winds. The two couples ran and crammed themselves into the dilapidated church building. What was left of the doors and windows provided very little shelter from the biting rain. Four of them stood crammed in a corner of the church. Using his dungaree shirt as cover, Brett rolled out a map and beckoned to the rest of the group who joined in to examine the map. The air was heavy and dark and suddenly, the atmosphere assumed a new seriousness devoid of banter. As soon as the rain stopped, they marched out in the direction indicated by Abenaa.

As they marched deeper into the forest, Mrs. Denning's anxiety started to get the better of her. For the past one week, she had seen and almost touched the much sought-after reed that was believed to hold the secret to her cure. That aspiration had been dashed the previous week by man's wanton destruction of the eco-system. The Konongo Gold Fields Corporation and the Konongo Timber and Plywood Corporation had destroyed her hope for a cure, when the two corporations wantonly ate up the forest that used to hold the curative plants that Sue needed so much.

Martin was intrigued at the silence and the look of heavy anxiety about the team as they marched deeper. into the forest; and as it opened into bright sunshine and a wide expanse of land. As they peered through the outcrop, they saw tractors and articulated trucks burrowing and ferrying sand endlessly. As they moved closer, they saw that what used to be a small River Seli, with little tributaries had been cleared open to swallow the adjoining streams and forests. They stared in awe at the gigantic civil works at the gigantic Bumbuna Hydroelectric Project.

Following initial inventory and feasibility studies by the UNDP and the World Bank in the Seventies and early eighties, the government of Sierra Leone had started site preparation work and excavation of the diversion tunnels on each side of the Seli River in 1982. Work continued on the project, even with the outbreak of the war; with the Italian government and the African Development Bank granting substantial loans. The Bumbuna Hydroelectric Project (BHP) located on the Seli River and the Sula mountains was half-way to completion when the RUF invaded and occupied the area as part of its push westwards towards Freetown as the civil war situation deteriorated.

The project which was abandoned all through the period of captivity of Martin and Brett in Camp 44 was designed to provide electricity to Freetown and the whole of the Western area of Sierra Leone; with inter-connections to other major provincial towns like Makeni, Lunsar, Kambia, Magburaka and Masiaka.

The two couples stared in awe at the huge rock-filled dam with asphalted concrete upstream face. A Y – shaped reservoir running for over a seventy miles long and over twelve miles in width had claimed all the adjoining forests, streams and fauna to the Seli River. Rare species of plants, reeds, reptiles, birds, and animals that were native to the Tinkololo forest simply disappeared to give way to the great dam. The large chimpanzee and boar population native to the forest either fled the area or were killed. In fleeing the niparian forest which had been their natural habitat for feeding, these and other primates in the area had become disorientated and extremely aggressive.

Abenaa stared in disbelief at the sheer emptiness of what used to be the Tonkolili forest; where she used to access a rich harvest of very rare plants; including the curative reed that had brought them back to Sierra Leone.Three years,just three years after their escape from Camp 44 and the huge reservoir of curative plants in the Tinkololo Forest was gone!! Beyond the Intake and Penstock areas, a giant powerhouse and generators were being installed above a huge turbine. Upstream, a further destruction of the eco-system had paved way for a large outflow river. Besides the destruction to the surrounding aquatic ecosystems, all the plants swallowed up by the giant reservoir and outflow river were decaying in an anaerobic environment, thereby forming and emitting dangerous green house gases, especially methane.

The choking sensation induced by methane and other green house gases forced the two couples back from the edge of the dam;and forced them into a hasty retreat. The two couples were speechless as they held on to each other in shock;and at the huge spectacle of ecological destruction that the dam had caused.The implication of the huge dam eating up the entire forest was all too clear to the couple as they were once again thrown into very sorrowful demeanors. Finally,it was Abenaa who had the courage to break the silence.... " It's alright... not to worry... Let's try the North Bank of the stream at Camp 44. I had seen the plant there sometime in the past also..." Abenaa said, as she broke the silence with words of hope. Sheepishly, with tears and sobs all round, they all swung round and followed Abenaa on the long march back to Camp 44.

As they were completing the long walk back to Camp 44, they were alarmed at the pulsating sound of whooshing air that billowed around the surrounding foliage. Looking through the trees, they saw a helicopter coming in to land. As the rotor blades slowed and the dust settled, they saw it was the same helicopter that had brought them that morning. But their extraction was not due until the next morning; so what was it doing back at Camp 44 so early?

As the doors pulled open, five white men dressed in khaki green dungarees; with infantry knapsacks and fully armed stepped out. The five men pushed out the pilot and co-pilot at gun- point.

"Hey... Captain Denning" one of them yelled out... "Come out right here... now!"

Brett looked at Martin in surprise. When they appeared to be hesitant, one of the five men fired a burst of AK47 round to hurry them up. As the couples came up to the five men, Martin challenged the apparent leader.

"What do you want from us?"

"I don't want anything from anyone for myself. I deliver results for anyone for a price"

"So what result do you seek... and for what price?. ""Come, talk to my boss... he needs the results... and he is paying the right price" As he spoke, he nudged the two couples toward the helicopter. There, at the rear of the helicopter, seated comfortably was the Camp 44 WHO liaison doctor, Doctor Bailey!

"My good friends" he chuckled as he stepped out of the helicopter.

"Did you really think you could enjoy the wealth from this medical discovery alone?" The two couples stared at each other in disbelief.

"Surprised? I have been tracking your movement since you left Camp 44. Was with you all the way in Ghana..."

Turning sharply to Abenaa, he spoke harshly.

"You don't play games with me... and don't tell me any African mythical secrecy stories about non – commercialization... Now... where is the plant? Search them!"

When the search revealed nothing, he turned to Martin and Brett.

"You know you are useless to me. You will just be two pieces of collateral damage." Doctor Bailey swung sharply to the five mercenaries.

"Take them away... shoot them if they don't co-operate" With that Brett and Martin were marched away.

"Now, my African Doctor, tell me, where is the plant?"

Calmly, Abenaa got close to him and spoke confidently.

"You are a disgrace to the medical profession. Is this the company you keep these days... all for money? What will you do with the money, when you make it? Can't you see you are being unreasonable... you think we would be here if we had the plant?"

"So where can we get the plant?" Doctor Bailey asked, now agitated and virtually pleading.

"Greedy people like you have killed the plant of life in the name of development. We were in Ghana in search of it... and powerful gold miners and timber corporations had destroyed it... Now we come to Sierra Leone and the huge new hydroelectric project out there on the Seli River has claimed it... a collateral damage of greedy people like you."

"So what do we do... where else can we turn to... to find this plant... we could be the richest people on earth if we can find it... can't you see?"

"Shut up! Yes, I say... shut your bloody trap up!" It was the frail voice of Sue Denning.

"You are such a disgrace. Does it matter to you that I am sick and dying and that I need that plant to revive me... and that is why this good lady is here... and not to make money like you... you are such a big disgrace"

"Don't get moralistic on me, young lady. You should have been this outspoken when your husband was whoring his life away in Freetown"

"Shut up! Shut up and leave Freetown out of this you bloody racist. And you call yourself a Doctor? What about the millions of people in your native Europe who are carrying the virus right now. Did they pick it from the air or from Freetown? You deserve the death that will surely come your way soon because of your greed."

"You are inconsequential" he said turning to Abenaa.

"Now, my African doctor, what do you say?

"There is one last chance... not for you but for the sake of my friend, Sue. Let's go, I saw the plant last on the bank of the stream up there" pointing to the North-bank of the Camp 44 stream. With that, they all moved in the direction of the stream. They forged the stream to the north bank and commenced a slow investigative march through the virgin eco-system. They marched for over three hours, with Abenaa making frequent stops to examine plants, stems, reeds and leaves.

As the only one in the party who knew exactly what plant they were looking for; she was priceless to everyone. She was in front leading the party when she spotted the plant on the route of a stream flowing down the mountain side. She saw the tall serrated leaves and the long delicate stem that held them about twenty meters away swaying to the wind: A smile of fulfilment lit up her lips as she turned... to announce her discovery to Martin. Just before she could open her mouth to share the priceless secret with anyone, several things happened at the same time.....

In the last one hour of their march through the jungle, any experienced tracker would have seen signs of Chimpanzee, boar and other primates. Their excreta and body odour loomed large. Killed in their thousands and displaced from the Seli River and Tonkolili forests in the course of the construction of the Bumbuna hydro-electric dam, the surviving boar and primate population had become suspicious of humans; and re-settled far away from human habitation on the north bank of the Camp 44 stream where they had become extremely protective of their habitat and extremely aggressive to human presence.

As the boar and primate population watched Abenaa and her team invade their habitat, images of the plunder that took place at the Tonkolili forest in the course of the construction of the Bumbuna Hydroelectric Project must have flashed through their minds. Without warning, three ferocious boars charged at the armed mercenary patrol, pushing straight for their groins. The surprise nature of the attack caught the mercenaries unaware. Before they could level their guns to fire, they had been floored, pinned down by their groins, struggling for survival. Their AK47s, primed in readiness on automatic fire assumed lives of their own and started firing indiscriminately. A stray bullet hit Abenaa in the head and she slumped without a sound, dead. Another bullet hit the co-pilot and Doctor Bailey.

With lightning speed, Brett and Martin took the AK47s from the fallen mercenaries and formed a defensive perimeter around the team. Briskly, they organized an orderly retreat with the casualties;firing sporadically to keep the ferocious animals at bay. A full charge by two boars and a group of chimpazees was cut short by a hail of automatic gunfire. Steadily, Brett and Martin organized a retreat across the stream, back to Camp 44 with the casualties.

It was already dark when they returned to the helicopter; and a catastrophic situation report: Abenaa dead! Doctor Bailey dead! Two mercenaries and the co-pilot dead! Amid uncontrollable, high-pitched wailing, tears and heavy hearts of sadness, a dazed and confused pilot managed to fly the survivors and casualties back to Freetown that night....to the Connaught Hospital.

With Abenaa dead, it was the end of the road. Brett, Martin and Sue did not realize how close they really were to the curative reed. They had been so near; yet so far from the much sought after curative reed!! Their return to Freetown that night was to mark the end of a long day. The end of a long journey. The end of a long desperate search for an alternative nature-based cure for the HIV pandemic. Yet, the end of another dream and a huge, backward step for Mankind.